Arthur Slade

Amber Fang

The Hunted

Contents

1

Feeding Day

My mother always told me never to fall in love with my food.

There was no chance of that today. Jordan Rex was not someone I—nor anyone with half an IQ point—would ever fall in love with. He *was* food, though. I could smell his blood from fifty feet away, the scent mingling with the alley's stink of dried urine and curdled milk.

I padded along on bare feet, the *Bachelorette*-style high heels I'd worn to the bar stuffed into my backpack purse. Stilettos were helpful in a waitress interview or on the dance floor, but hunting shoes they're not. I scanned for security cameras. The blurred images of me feeding in Boston had forced the move to Seattle. I was already deathly sick of the constant drizzle.

Mr. Rex was wobble-weaving a path farther and farther down the alley into sketchy territory—buildings with broken windows, a few rusted fire escapes hanging loosely on the walls, no lights in any of the windows. He stood at least six feet four, so he had a good eight inches on me, and he boasted enormous arms. For a forty-five-year-old, he was carrying very little flab. Still, easy pickings. As long as I did everything right, that is.

Slow and steady. Mom had drilled that command into me ad

infinitum. *Your prey must never suspect your presence. Become the wind.*

She actually did say that. Every time. Then she'd giggle and touch the tip of her petite nose to show she was joking. I inherited that same nose, but not the nose-tapping habit. She was an odd bird. And I loved her to bits.

In most vampire movies, the prey suffers long minutes of terror. They scream. They beg. They die. Not so in the real world—my world, that is. It's not efficient hunting. The best kills are silent and over before the food knows it's dead, before their fight-or-flight response kicks in. An overtaxed heart makes the blood spurt with too much force. I'd wrecked a perfectly good white dress that way, a few months back.

Something whirred in the air far above me, but I couldn't see exactly what might be making that sound and was too hungry to care.

My gray eyes provided handy night vision. Rex was a red outline in the alley. Soon, he'd be outlined in chalk, and some poor cop would be trying to write up his case. Those suckers didn't get paid enough.

Suckers. Ha!

Choose your food carefully, Mom had taught me. My moral imperative was not to kill innocents. This was the hunting criterion Mom had drilled into my DNA. The food must be a murderer.

Rex hadn't been my first choice this month. At the start of this feeding cycle, I'd been tracking a man named Timothy Huxton and had fully intended to dine on him last Thursday. But the day before feeding day, he'd made the ninety-ninth call to KISW and won a two-week vacation to Mazatlán. My mouth watered as I thought of how much better he'd taste with

2

a tan.

So I'd rushed to uncover Jordan Rex's lethal backstory, flipping through archived newspapers in the glass monstrosity known as the Seattle Public Library (my library science classes were coming in handy). I discovered him in the transcripts of a ten-year-old murder trial. Two wives dead in less than two years. Both judged as death by misadventure. I knew better.

We were getting closer to the docks. Waves crashed, and the occasional mournful foghorn moaned. Rex came to a dead end. He ambled right up to the wire fence blocking the alley—some sort of storage space. He stumbled against it, and the chain links rattled.

I took my first step into the open, and he turned and looked directly at me. "It's about time you showed up," he said. He didn't slur a single word.

I hesitated in mid-crouch. He knew I was following him? I could question him, but mom's voice came into my head: *Never play with your food.* I leapt forward with more speed than any human was capable of and reached out to grab Rex's shoulder and dip him down for feeding. At that exact microsecond, a *puff puff pop* came from above. I felt as if I'd been rabbit punched twice in the back and kicked in the leg.

I turned. Darts stuck out of my right shoulder and my lower back. Darts! Who used darts in this day and age? Another quivered in my thigh. The whirring in the sky grew slightly louder.

I fell forward. Rex opened his arms like a lecherous uncle. I gathered enough strength to throw myself toward the fence. I bounced off. My leg collapsed, and I skidded across the ground. My vision blurred. I pushed myself up, tried to run, and stumbled right into an inhospitable brick wall. I lay on my back, blinking.

One of those little four-bladed drones was peeking over the roof of the building. Someone with an iPhone and a night vision app was probably lining me up in its crosshairs.

"Hit her again," Rex commanded. The drone exhaled another *puff puff pop*. Two darts zipped down, ricocheting off the pavement. The third one stung my left shoulder.

I shrugged it off and climbed to my feet. "Who. Are. You?"

"I'm a party who's very interested in your activities." He walked slowly toward me, pulling at something inside his coat. *I'm a party, I'm a party* echoed inside my head. What was in those darts?

I lurched ahead and shoved him to the ground, briefly catching a lemony-antiseptic scent. Then I latched onto the fence and pulled myself up about three feet. Rex grabbed my ankle, but I managed a feeble kick and through blind luck, connected with his head. He let out a satisfying groan (well, satisfying to me) and stepped back. I climbed higher, my fingers now icicles, fell over the other side, and thudded unceremoniously to the ground. On a normal day, with normal reflexes, I could leap right over that six feet of wire. Instead, I crawled away.

"Oh, I'll do it myself," Rex huffed behind me. He had drawn a gun.

I dug my nails into a slimy brick wall and pulled myself up. By the sounds of footsteps and metallic clinking behind me, big ol' Rex was climbing the fence.

I pushed aside a pile of crates and discovered a boarded-up window. Luck was with me! I launched myself through the rotten wood and ran down a hall through the semi-darkness. Trash. Broken chairs. A multitude of blurry red, rat-shaped

4

outlines fled from me.

I brushed by a mannequin with a dozen bullet holes in it. Then I stumbled into a larger room. My left eye was beginning to fail, blinking with blinding tears. The eyelid cemented shut. I kept banging into things I thought were several feet away. But I ran at full speed, ignoring the pain.

By the crashing and swearing behind me, it was clear Rex was in the building. Humans were such loud, bashing creatures—I never got how they survived the hunter-gatherer phase. At least the drone wouldn't be able to operate in such close quarters. I stumble-ran through a gaping hole in the wall into another building, then another. More rats scattered before my feet.

I kept pushing ahead as quietly as possible. My brain slowed, and my right eye was drooping now. Soon I'd be blind.

Half the cells in my body were shouting *sleep* and the other half were screaming *need blood feed now.* The sleep cells were winning the battle, so when I spotted a pile of stained, dusty sheets that may have been used for wiping up vomit after a meth party, I jittered toward them. I saw my mother ahead of me wagging her finger and saying, *Now Amber, how many times do I have to tell you not to be overconfident?*

Shut it, Mom. You're not helping.

That's no way to talk to the vampire who gave birth to you.

I wouldn't be in this situation if you hadn't left.

That shut her up. I pulled the sheets over me. By this time, my right eye had fused shut, and I didn't know if I was lying there half exposed. I promptly fell into a deep, dark pit of unconsciousness.

******

5

When I came to there was a light grayness to my vision, and I wondered if I'd developed cataracts. A sight-impaired vampire having to beg food to *come just a little bit closer* is the saddest thing under the sun.

I remembered I was lying under a sheet. I pulled a corner away, and the sun glared through a broken window, stabbing into my eyes. I had to blink. Despite that, a smile came to half of my face. The other half was frozen. I hoped the darts hadn't given me a stroke.

My skin didn't burn with the sun's rays. It wouldn't. That was an old wives' tale. Or an *old guy with too much time on his hands* tale. I'd burn if I was out in the sun too long, but most things with skin do. That's why I wore sunblock.

The people who'd attacked me obviously didn't have dogs. Not that the canines would've been able to track my mostly negligible scent. But some dogs, well, they just didn't know when to quit.

I listened. Nothing but ship sounds coming through the window. It may have opened directly onto the docks. Seagulls cried out for food. I sniffed. Old paint, old piss, and several other smells, but not a human pheromone that wasn't already a few weeks old. My pursuers hadn't even entered this room.

How had I become the hunted?

The man had known I was tracking him and had obviously set up a trap. And they'd used a drone. Not a sniper. I would've seen the heat outline of a man. So they had guessed how my vision worked. And they'd fired darts. Darts! Like I was some sort of tiger to be knocked out and trussed up for a zoo. But any tranquilizers that would work on humans wouldn't necessarily work on me, though Scotch does, oddly enough. I have a different metabolism. In fact, sometimes tranquilizers were like a massive hit of adrenaline to my body. Yet these people had nearly captured me. So they most likely knew I wasn't human.

It was embarrassing when your food outsmarted you. I should've known that Rex was too easy to dig out of the archives.

But the fact they were able to set this up was rather frightening. They had either planted evidence or taken over the life of this Rex character. Was it a coincidence that my first meal had won a trip to Mexico? I shuddered at the thought, because if they had rigged the contest, it meant, whoever they were, they had money and a bigger team than Rex and the drone boy. The commanding tone of the man's voice suggested they had connections to the police or to a military organization. The drone had been whisper quiet—sophisticated high tech. And you don't just find tranquilizer darts at the local grocer. To hunt me down while I hunted them, to know my practices, that all reeked of researchers. An organization.

Blood. Blood.

Hunger was still rattling my nerves. I'd need to eat in the next twenty-four hours. I did not want to collapse. Or go on a frenzied blood drive. A packet from the hospital would never work. It had to be fresh blood drawn from the jugular—at least, that's what tasted the best.

I heard my mother's voice lovingly say, *Always have a backup meal.*

7

2

The Backup Meal

The Washington State Penitentiary in Walla Walla, Washington is not an easy place to break into when you've had time to plan, but it's especially hard when you're in a rush for blood. I took the train from Seattle to Portland, then east, tapping my fingers all the way to the Amtrak station in Pasco. Eleven hours of travel. I tried not to stare at the jugulars on my fellow passengers' necks.

The hunger jangled my nerves, sharpened my incisors, and slowly turned my thoughts crimson. *Do not ever go thirty days without eating*—this was Mom's biggest rule—or *you'll become mad as a hatter.* When I was a kid, I imagined dancing crazily with a floppy top hat on. In reality, I'd go on a frantic killing spree, gorging indiscriminately on humans—deserving and undeserving—and most likely be shot full of lead by a SWAT team. Vampires were averse to seeing their own blood.

It was extremely hard to sit still in a moving pen of your food. But turning this into a dining car would be too messy, far too public, and bad for my figure. I could hold on.

My backpack had my favorite things in it: a few dark shirts, three pairs of stretchy pants, one nice set of clothes, and a picture of my mother and me. Nothing electronic so I could avoid being tracked by some invisible app.

Taking the train always reminded me of Mom. We had taken a lot of trains together. And buses. And cabs. And airplanes.

We ran; that was our habit. We changed homes every year or so. Sometimes there would be something in the press about one of our hunts. But other times, my mom just got spooked. She'd pull me from school (I did grade six in five states), throw me into our station wagon stuffed with all our clothes and books, and we'd race several states away. I sometimes got the feeling it wasn't just humans we were running away from.

One day, I came home from school and she was gone. *Out on a feed* her note had said. *Be back after lunch.* She'd used a raspberry magnet to stick it to the refrigerator door. When she was three hours late, I knew something had happened. I watched the internet and listened to our police scanner for any mention of her fate. Not a word. I waited in our apartment even though the protocol was to run if there had been several hours without contact.

I tapped my fingers for three days. Then I grabbed my passport and my backpack and tracked down her intended meal—a man who had murdered his cousin for a sandwich. He was still alive, which meant she hadn't fed. I questioned him, but he had no knowledge of Mom.

I ate him and moved to Chicago. I've been moving ever since.

I was first out the door of the train and first into a cab. Somewhere close to midnight, I found myself standing outside the concrete walls of the Washington State Penitentiary.

It was surrounded by fields. It had towers. Barbed wire. And the latest in motion detectors. And, of course, stereotypical, straight-jawed men with high-powered rifles at all four corners of the prison with perfect sight lines to the lovely interior. I swallowed, then licked my lips. I was in a black yoga outfit that made it easier to hide.

I climbed the conning tower, swung over the wall, and crossed the yard in the shadows. Prison staff didn't normally look for people who were breaking *in*.

I followed a guard into the building. He had enough neck and ear hair to keep a team of waxers in business for a lifetime. With every beat of my heart, my body called for blood. His blood was not out of the question. I memorized the back of his neck. I also slipped a set of keys from his belt.

It became very hard to concentrate the moment I entered the building and smelled the sweaty pheromones of all the living blood producers trapped in prison cells. Soon any transgressor would fit my criteria. *You're in here for an ounce of weed? Sorry, Dude, a gal's gotta eat.*

I moved more slowly than usual. I blamed it on the after-effects of the tranquilizer. *It must be a murderer*, my mother had repeated right up until the day she vanished from my life. *Never the innocent. That's our moral code. Blood for blood. Life for life. And the murderer must not have remorse.*

That last little caveat was a doozy. It was devilishly hard to sort out who felt remorse and who faked it. Humans were experts at faking a whole rainbow of emotions.

It took me an hour to work my way into death row. I salivated the whole time. Several times, I had to climb the walls and turn cameras away from me. I can crawl into holes most humans would never imagine as crawlable spaces. Bones that compressed and bent were so handy.

Eventually, I came to cell block six and found the massive metal door that led to Percival Horpon's cell. He'd bludgeoned three old ladies to death over the course of an evening ten years earlier. He had no motive, not even theft, though he did keep their hearing aids and false teeth as trophies. He'd been officially classified a serial killer, and well, we all knew the amount of remorse a serial killer felt. I had kept his records in my mental back pocket in case I ever needed a quick feed. I generally didn't like breaking into prisons to do this sort of thing because he would never be a public threat.

None of the keys I'd stolen worked. Why was nothing easy? I'm strong, but I couldn't tear off the reinforced door.

So I went back to the guard station. It was empty—perhaps it was union break time. There I found an ancient computer and, after changing the screen from a game of pong, found the program for the electromechanical locks and opened his cell. Nearly every prison system used the same computer program, and it was quite hackable. These were the sorts of things librarians learned.

When I went back, the door was partly open. Percival was still snoring. I crept in and identified a distinguishing tattoo on his lovely, thick neck—a black widow spider.

I must have been overtired because when I went to turn his head for a better angle, he shot straight up and said, "Whodafuk?" I grabbed his Mohawk with one hand and his shoulder with the other and bit somewhere in between, but I didn't get good suction, so blood went spurting into my eye, onto the white sheets, and halfway across the cell.

"Gettoffme!" He half shouted. His life squirted out in red arcs.

Dammit! Dammit! Dammit!

I tightened my grip, but my hands were slick with redness. He smacked me with a punch to the forehead. I took a second bite but was knocked back by another fist. Now there were four little fountains of red.

Mom would kill me if she saw this mess.

I dug my claws into his arms and stabbed my incisors right below his tattooed spider. And got good suction. Horpon dropped his arms and went still.

The bite of a vampire secretes a paralytic agent along with an anticoagulant. Paralysis occurs in less than a second.

Always finish your meal. Mom had repeated this several thousand times.

I had to keep draining the blood until my food expired. There was a chemical release on death. At least, that was the way Mom explained it; it wasn't like we had any textbooks. The chemical was acetylcholine, and it told my brain I'd finished eating and reset my clock. If I didn't feed all the way to my dinner's death, then my thirty-day clock didn't get reset, and an uncontrollable bloodlust could flick on at any time. Cue the crimson insanity. Cue the cops hunting me down. Cue my death.

When I was done, I wiped my face and whispered, "Thank you, Mr. Horpon, for offering up your life." He didn't reply.

I often slept after dining, but if I was caught snoring beside my deceased food, it would cause a hubbub. I snuck out of the prison the way I'd come in.

I washed the blood off my face in a babbling brook a thousand yards from the prison, retrieved my hidden backpack, then walked into Walla Walla and hopped a late bus to another country.

3

Settling In

Three days and three train rides later, I was renting an apartment in Montréal, Canada. The suite was in a building that had been poorly designed in the 1950s and not improved on since. But the location was ideal—a few blocks from the Université de Montréal, where I could continue my library science degree. I could speak passable French, which I'd picked up a few years earlier in Louisiana. I was working hard to erase the creole sayings I'd been taught, including *Lâche pas la patate*, which loosely translated to, "Don't let go of the potato." In other words: be obstinate. The Québécois tended to turn up their collective noses to such quaintness.

Food should never turn its nose up to me.

I chose an identity I hadn't used for ages: Amber Tyrell. I hadn't used my real first name for a few years, and it felt good to bring it back into circulation. I was me again.

Mom had put the passport together three years earlier. I still matched the photograph perfectly. Twenty-four years on this planet, but I didn't look a day over twenty-one and wouldn't for another thirty years.

I didn't know much more about the longevity of my kind.

Mom said her grandmother had lived to be two hundred five and only died when a train hit her. Alzheimer's had done it. Well, technically, the train did it, but Alzheimer's had made her go on a meandering walk. Old Japetha Fang had thought the light coming toward her was an angel. It was not.

I believed I'd be more difficult to track down if I moved half a continent and a whole country away. Neither the FBI nor the CIA played nice with the Canadian Security Intelligence Service. I still sweated when I thought of the drone and those tranquilizer darts.

Things had been easier when Mom was here to guide me. To guide us, that is.

I spent two hours at a computer in the public library, digging around the registrar's codes, tapping my finger so hard I chipped the granite tabletop. When I finally cracked the password, I was able to insert my name into enough classes to fill out my semester. My goal was to finish my Master's degree, find a quiet job as a librarian in a populated place, and spend my time researching my meals and trying to track down Mom. Her trail was frozen. But we Fangs didn't let go of the potato so easily.

The last name Fang was pretty much all I knew about my family. Heck, I didn't even know my father. Whenever I would ask about him, Mom would give me that familiar strained smile. "Oh, he was a pair of teeth and not much more."

She had been a wizard with investments. The consistent windfalls provided me with a modest-enough sum to live a frugal yet tasteful life. I did occasionally get a student loan. Easy to do when you just changed your name to avoid paying it back.

The next morning, I took a bus to the Université de Montréal.

A phallic bell tower loomed over the campus, and the buildings were done in a yellow brick, art deco style. It was not beautiful, but it felt permanent.

I strode down the hall and sat in the back row of an elective I'd chosen: *Comparative History of Socio-Religious Mentalities*. The room stank of too much perfume on the women and coffee breath and underarm effluvia on the men. To be fair, the women had coffee breath too. But why was it that some men didn't shower before a morning class? It would have made the world a much more beautiful place. Smell-wise, that is.

Professor Slemay was one of those humans who'd been gifted with a nasally voice and an obnoxious ability to eviscerate his students. Some professors were there to teach; others to prove their superiority to the rest of humanity.

"How about you, Mademoiselle Tyrell?" he asked in French.

It took me a moment to remember that Tyrell was my last name. "Yes, monsieur," I said.

"I would like to know your opinion of the French Revolution. In particular, the economic situation that precipitated it."

"Oh, I wouldn't lose my head over it," I said.

This got a bit of snicker from my classmates. As jaded as I was, I did love the sound of human laughter. Slemay's measuring eyes and his measuring brain made a check mark beside my name. He was also holding his ledger white-knuckle tight.

"Well, Mizz Tyrell," he said. "I was looking for an answer with depth."

"I am not deep ... but I'm very wide. That's a Balzac quote, by the way." I was drawing attention to myself. *Don't stand out.* Mom's words. But Professor Slemay was so pompous. So ... so *human*! "I'm a little behind on my reading, sir. I've only just begun attending your extraordinary class. Perhaps you would

15

like to ask one of my fellow students?"

"I judge my students by their ability to prepare for class," he said.

My dander was up, along with the hairs on the back of my neck. Old food should not talk to me this way. I pointed at him. "The economics of the time can be summed up in one word: greed. The nobility lived tax free. The peasants and the bourgeoisie did not. The country was deep in debt from the Seven Years' War and from supporting the American Revolution. The French Revolution came about because of the pressure put on the lower classes. Raise the taxes enough, and eventually the masses begin building guillotines." Apparently my dander was dandered to the max because I just couldn't stop myself. "Does the brain inside the decapitated head die immediately, or does it have thoughts for a few seconds? Professor Slemay, what did Marie Antoinette think in those seconds and was it deeper than your thoughts right now?"

He stared at me with dead lizard eyes. "That's a notable answer." He made a notation in his ledger.

My mother was hissing in the back of my head. *Stand down. Stand down.*

I'd made an enemy. And I'd broken one of Mom's laws. But the approving glances I got from my fellow students made me feel slightly better.

I began searching for my dinner right after class. I had twenty-five days before I'd have to feed again, and I was looking forward to dining on my first Canadian, or Québécois, as they called themselves here. I wondered if they'd taste a bit maple syrupy, perhaps with a soupçon of rubber hockey puck.

I made my first trip to the courthouse on *Rue Notre-Dame* to stick my nose into transcripts of court cases. Montréal had its share of gangs—Rock Machine and Hells Angels being the most notable. The polite Canadian stereotype did not apply to those tattooed ruffians. I didn't like feeding on organized crime. I'd spent some time hunting down members of the Mafia in Boston. Being shot by a henchman was a very unpleasant experience. I healed quickly, but bullets still hurt. A lot. And a headshot would take me out. At least, I'm pretty certain it would. I didn't want to know what type of gray matter might grow back after my brains had been blown out. And, even when you got your kill done, the police had an annoying habit of becoming extremely interested. Two fang holes did tend to arouse suspicions. I've read their reports about the vampire hit man.

Hit man! How that frosted my feminist heart.

I did have to admit, it was an adrenaline rush when you're hunting food that fought back. *It's not curiosity that killed the cat,* Mom would say, *it's adrenaline.*

I dug up an old lady who'd murdered four husbands and hadn't spent a moment behind bars. I could smell her guilt on the papers. But there had been several articles about her in the major papers and a documentary on the Canadian Broadcasting Corporation. When she died, it would make the national news.

Ah, she wouldn't work. Nose to grindstone again.

I read. And read. The Canadians didn't kill each other as often as my fellow Americans. Perhaps they got all of their aggression out at hockey games.

I've been on this earth for twenty-four years. According to my calculations, I've had to research and hunt down one hundred sixty-eight meals. Sometimes I find the process a little boring.

I should point out that for the first two years of my life, I was breastfed. And that from ages three to eleven, my mother did all the research to feed us. Oh, and she brought me my dinner.

17

It was very touching. And a lot of blood for me to handle. I'd sometimes sleep for three days after a meal. But at age thirteen, it became my job to find my morally agreeable food. We all had our chores to do.

I found no good leads the first day. There would be time. Human beings, even polite ones, liked to kill each other. And many didn't feel remorse. It was in their nature.

It was in my nature to eat them.

4

Finding My Meal

I fell into that all too familiar student life pattern: studying for classes, writing essays in the library, and returning to my apartment to read for pleasure. I never watched TV. I preferred words on paper. I bought a wooden rocking chair, and it became my reading chair. Mom used to rock me to sleep every night and stroke my hair, so I found the motion comforting. I put the picture of Mom and me on my mantel.

My French became more passable, and day-by-day, I adjusted my accent so it didn't sound so Louisianan. I dropped all the creole, though I would miss saying *Bon-temps fait crapaud manqué bounda*—which we all know means, "Idleness leaves the frogs without buttocks." They'd been speaking their own French here for about three hundred years. I learned to imitate it.

I continued to hunt for dinner.

I didn't want a young victim. They hadn't had time to be remorseful, which sometimes came with age. I stationed myself in the courthouse library and dug through old documents. I did love research. My life depended on it, and so studying for my Master's had turned my brain into a highly efficient research machine. And no one ever suspected librarians of anything beyond saying *shush*. When's the last time a good murder was committed by a librarian? We'd rather read about it.

I went through index cards—yes, they still had index cards—and finally unearthed the story of a woman who had poisoned her parents in 1950: Claudette Finnegan. She'd inherited a goodly sum and only spent twelve years in prison. According to my math, she would be nearly eighty-five-years-old. She might be dead.

I did some more sifting and discovered she was very much alive and very, very rich. She even owned a share in the Montréal Canadiens, and lived in a top floor condo on St. Catherine Street.

I used some clever magic to find her phone number, which meant I looked it up in an old copy of the phone book. I dialed the number. "Bonjour," she said.

"This is Sarah Coxwell. You don't know me."

"No, I don't, and I'm about to hang up."

"Ah, one moment, please! I'm a psychology student at Université de Montréal. And I wonder … have you ever felt any remorse about your parents' murders?"

"Excuse me?" she said.

"I'm studying the effect of time on remorse. Since no remorse was declared in the trial, did you develop any contrition as time passed?"

"You're brave. Clap yourself on the back. Ask me what's in my right hand."

"What's in your right hand?"

A raspy chuckle followed. "A glass of champagne. I've had one every day for sixty years. I live in a world where others make my meals and bring them to me. Lobster one day, tapas the next."

"Are you implying you haven't developed any remorse?"

"I am saying that I enjoy these fine things in life. I did not enjoy my parents. Put that in your thesis, child. Most parents live far too long."

"Thank you, Mrs. Finnegan. You won't believe how much you've helped me."

She laughed. It was not light-hearted. "My pleasure. Have a nice day, sweetheart."

I had my next meal.

5

A New Slab of Food

Time passed. An old lady died. There was very little press other than an obituary in the *Montréal Gazette*.

And in my ever-present need to stay under the radar, I kept a steady row of B+'s to my name, just below the dean's list. My mouth remained shut in Comparative History class. When Professor Slemay asked me a question, I could sense people waiting for my clever reply, but I expressed only blandness. The expectations of my fellow students dropped.

I was beginning to feel slightly safe.

A new slab of male food walked into my *GLIS 645: Archival Principles and Practices* class. He had either signed up quite late, or his attendance had been severely spotty. He sat a row over from me. He was handsome, had a skull earring in his right ear, a square cut to his jaw, and a confidence in his eyes. Most of the men studying to become librarians weren't alpha males, but he clearly was. His hair was wavy yet short. His heart was beating seventy-seven times per minute. I could separate the sound it made from all the other beating hearts in the classroom. I glanced up at him, took in all this information, and looked away.

We were well into the argument about the benefits and detractions of the ICA standard, ISO standard, and DIRKS standard, and the discussion was getting rather heated. By that, I mean a woman who was wearing 1950s-era glasses was sub-vocalizing about why she loved DIRKS. I kept my mouth shut. I'm an ISO girl, through and through.

When class was over, I headed toward the bus stop. Only a few steps into the journey, I noted that someone was following me. Even without turning I could guess the weight (197 pounds) and the sex (male, but it was mostly the weight that determined that). I took a path to my left, and he followed.

I slowed down, and in a move that would look like I was falling, I flipped against the wall and extended my leg to trip him.

He hopped over my proffered leg. It was alpha boy from class. He shot me a questioning look.

"Sorry," I said. "I stumbled."

"Are you okay?" he asked. He had a Louisianan twang to his French.

"I'm fine. Were you following me?"

"Following you?" He wiped at the sweat on his forehead. "I was trying to catch up with you."

"Why?" I asked. I kept my voice cool. You showed the slightest bit of interest in a man, and they interpreted it as an open invitation to a night of romping.

"Your notes."

"My notes?"

He nodded. "I hope it's not too much of a bother, but I've been sick and would appreciate catching up."

"Did you ask Mary Lemieux in the third row? She's a much more meticulous note taker."

"No. I didn't. I was only interested in your notes."

I switched to English. "You wanted to talk to me, you mean?"

He switched to English without batting an eye. "Well, yes. If that's a by-product of getting your notes."

By-product? Nerd alert! "Where'd you get that accent?"

"Louisiana. I grew up there." His eyes were gray. This was the longest conversation I'd had with anyone for at least a year. "I have a cousin who lives in Montréal. I recognized your accent too. You only spoke once today, but it was enough." Damn! I'd worked hard to stamp out that twang. "Quiet as a mouse, aren't you? But I bet there's a lot going on inside your head."

Did he think I'd roll over at the first compliment? Although, I must say, my smile was genuine. "You can tell that?"

"I have a knack for 'getting' people's personalities. Anyway, about your notes."

"Sure. I'll share them." There was a cleft in his chin. His jugular was very attractive. If it'd been later in the month, I would've been staring at it.

He held out his hand for a shake. "Dermot."

Despite my instinct, I took his hand. It was a strong grip. "Dermot? Really? Your parents lose a bet to an Irish man?"

His laugh was genuine. As I mentioned before, I did like the sound of human laughter. "They wanted to reflect our Irish roots. Not that any of us have set foot in Ireland in the last hundred years. And your name?"

"Amber." I did get a sniff of him, and his scent wasn't quite there. It was as if the sweetly scented aftershave was hiding another smell. On purpose. A tiny tendril of suspicion niggled in my brain.

"Well, I really appreciate the leg up," he said.

"What's your number?" I said. "I'll text the notes to you." We exchanged digits. I gave him a dummy number that'd forward messages to my main account. My notes were actually on my iPad, but I didn't want to dig it out of my backpack. "Well," I said. "Nice talking to you, Dermot."

"Wait." He reached for my arm, but my withering glance stopped him. I was rather adept at withering glances. "Would you like to get something to eat?"

"I don't do breakfast," I said. "See you in Archival Practices." Then I turned and walked away. There was something mechanical about his movements. As if he'd acted out this scene. It could be he was actually shy. Most boys didn't approach me. Yes, a few of the jocks. But they would back down at the bar when I flashed my virtual fangs. Not my real ones, of course. Those only came out once a month. Maybe he'd rehearsed this little tête-à-tête in his dorm room a hundred million times.

No. This was the first time he'd met me.

His smell. It didn't hit me until I was a few steps away. But it hit me hard.

Beneath the sweet scent was the same lemon-scented anti-septic I'd sniffed on my attacker in Seattle.

He was one of them. I stopped but didn't turn around.

"Did you change your mind?" he asked. "A little breakfast would go a long way."

I'd have to kill him.

Survival trumps all rules. That was written right at the bottom of my mom's list. On a campus of twenty thousand people, it wouldn't be easy to find a dark corner. But humans weren't very observant. Plus, I could do it quickly, but then I'd have to move again. I wouldn't even be able to go back to my apartment. Agents would be watching it—I was pretty certain of that. I always kept a spare passport in my purse. Maybe I would head to Europe. Spain was nice this time of year—well, any time of year.

It would be good to question him though. My delicate ears didn't pick up any buzzing of a drone.

"So, do you have grumblies in your tumbly?" he asked.

Grumblies in your tumbly? Was he Winnie the Pooh? I slowly turned. Best to just kill him right here. Then flee. *Keep it Simple Stupid*, Mom used to always say.

"Yes," I said. "I've changed my mind."

He was grinning. And handsome. A shame to waste the blood, but I gained no advantage from feeding this early in the month.

"I'm nutso for pancakes." There was such confidence in his voice. He had a backpack, but his pants were too tight to hide a weapon. Unless he had a gun tucked in his belt right above his butt. The jacket was long enough to cover that. An awkward place to reach. And I could react faster than him.

We were still alone, brick walls on either side of us. No witnesses were peering down through the windows.

Best to break his neck and throw him through a darkened basement window. I'd have maybe a few hours before he was discovered. Or I could toss him down a manhole. Then I'd have a week.

I shot my hand out, but when it was an inch from his neck, he grabbed me by the wrist.

Impossible. No human could move fast enough to stop me.

"Please," he said. "Don't start this dance."

Had he just gotten lucky with that grab? I whipped up my other hand, and he caught it. I twisted out of his grip, but not easily.

I aimed a kick at his knee. He blocked it.

"You can't have my notes, Dermot," I said.

Then I sprinted away.

When I glanced back, I saw he was following with a big fat Cheshire Cat grin.

6

The Pursuit

I bumped past students and knocked over professors, moving at a blurring speed. Through the courtyard. Down a trail. Then we were on the street, outracing cars. He kept pace. He actually kept pace. I dodged down a side street.

This was aggravatingly curious. One part of my mind was figuring out which car to dodge, which fence to leap over, and scanning the sky for drones; another part was enjoying the exhilaration of running freely at full speed—something I rarely did in view of humans. A third inquisitive section of my brain was trying to figure out exactly how alpha boy was matching my speed. Not even an Olympic sprinter should be able to do that.

A fourth part of my mind was panicking. Because I was the pursued. Again. My heart beat slightly faster than it should, and my palms were sweaty. This was what prey felt like. I was not prey. I was never meant to be prey. Being at the top of the food chain, I took that for granted. I deserved respect.

Anger began to broil in my chest.

Well, he could run. I gave him that. He certainly didn't seem to be breaking much of sweat. Each time I glanced back, he was still grinning. Though—if my eyes weren't deceiving me—his grin was not as wide and mocking as it had been a few blocks earlier. We dashed across a park, doves flap-scattering before us.

Then I led him down *Avenue Gatineau* and into an alley that smelled like Chinese food. There was a tall, windowless, brick wall directly in front of me, so I decided to see if he could climb.

I leapt up and scaled the wall. I am light and my nails are sharp and nigh unbreakable, so I clung easily to most anything. I gouged out a few chunks of brick and mortar. Not quite with the ease of Spider-Man, but still mildly awe-inspiring. About thirty feet up, I stopped and turned my head.

Dermot was below me. He jumped, launching his frame remarkably high, but nowhere near where I was. He grabbed for a brick. It broke under his weight, and he fell with an *umph*.

I rotated so that I was upside down staring at him. "You look stupid jumping."

"I suppose I do. Plus, it's hard on the ankles. Not to mention the ego."

"Who are you?" I asked. "I mean, is Dermot really your name?"

"Yeah, it is." He grinned. "Why don't you come down and chat face to face."

"Why don't you come up?"

"Not possible. That's a nice trick. Are your hands sticky or something?"

"No. I think you've mistaken me for someone who'll answer your questions." Of course, I just had; stupid me. "Why are you chasing me?"

"To talk."

"You enrolled in library studies and pursued me halfway

across Montréal to chat?"

"I also flew across the country into a foreign land. That's how important this chat is to me."

"Well, we're talking now, Dermot. Answer me this: why are you so fast?"

"That's classified."

"You'll have to do better than that, Dermot."

"You don't seem to like my name, Amber."

"There's a lot I don't like about you. For instance, who do you work for? Why are you chasing me? Actually, just leave me alone. I don't need any new friends."

He nodded. "I did suspect you were antisocial, but I didn't realize to what extent. Do you have any friends at all?"

"I don't make friends with food." I hadn't meant to say that. But I guessed he knew more about me than ... well ... anyone, other than my mother. "Where's my mom?" That just came out. "Do you have her?"

He scratched at his curly hair. "No. I was not aware you had a mother."

Oh great, I'd given him more information.

He cleared his throat, then he actually said, no lie, "I have a mission for you."

"Is this a joke?"

"No. I've been studying you for four years. We have intuited several things about you and your personality. And I ..." He rubbed his neck. "Listen, my neck is getting sore."

"I hope your head falls off."

"Couldn't we have a coffee? Do you drink coffee? I mean, I know you don't have to, but maybe you just like the caffeine."

"It makes me aggressive."

"Okay, no coffee then." He put his palms up. "What if I

promised not to harm you?"

"What if I promised not to pluck off your arms?"

"Those are terms I could agree to." He drew in a deep breath. "I really am here to talk, Amber. Nothing else. You can walk away at any time. You must be curious though. Aren't you just a little?"

He had me there. "Don't move." I spat the words out.

I flipped around and dropped down, landing about ten feet away from him. Silently, I might add. The flip was just for show, and I must admit I was pleased by how it had turned out. "Talk," I said. "Now."

"No tea? Or orange juice?"

"You don't want me to drink my favorite drink."

"Point taken. Well, Amber, we've been interested in you for some time now."

"Who is we?"

"An unnamed organization."

I rubbed my neck. "Can you at least give me an acronym?"

"We don't really have one. We're just ... well, we're like a guild."

"A knitting guild?"

"Look, we're here to help."

I laughed. "I don't need help."

"You aren't the only vampire, you know. You aren't alone."

Well, duh, I wanted to say. My mom was a vampire. And so was my father. But beyond that, I knew very little. So he had me there.

"Fine," I said. "Let's go for a drink. You'll be doing the drinking. My choice of establishment."

There was a coffee spot a few doors up called *Brûlerie St-Denis*, in one of those quaint old buildings that peppered Montréal. He hadn't come with a gun or darts or a drone, so perhaps he would be worth talking to. And I *was* curious. He actually opened the door for me, and we found a table.

"Why do you say I'm not alone?" I asked, once we'd sat down.

"Tea first," he said. And he was off to the counter. He was more broad-shouldered than I'd first noticed.

He came back with two cups of steaming tea in his hands, sat, and placed one in front of me.

"Your tea is just for show," he said. "We know you're not alone because we've found others."

"How many?"

"That's classified."

"Is it a number higher than ten?"

He shrugged. "Now, let's talk about you. And the value of your services."

"My services?"

"You have the ability to get in and out of places that are impenetrable to most humans. The prison at Walla Walla is a fine example. I spent an inordinate amount of time watching those security tapes. I think I saw your shadow at one point. You're extremely gifted."

"It's mostly genetic. And good training."

"My organization is a guild of like-minded people who prefer to operate without government involvement for the betterment of the democratically elected world."

A whole bunch of alarm bells went off. "Sounds cozy. And imperialistic. How do you decide who the bad guys are?"

"Let's say there are people who ... well ... for the good of the world, shouldn't be breathing. These are the people whom we would like you to kill."

"For which country?"

"America. We're the good guys. Well, us and Canada, the UK, France, and Lithuania."

"That's an eclectic group." I watched him sip his tea and waited until he set the cup down before I spoke. "No. I won't have someone else pick my food for me."

"Food. Is that how you classify us?"

"Yes."

"Do you think that's a way of shutting yourself off from your connection to humans?"

"I have no connection to humans other than consumption. Oh, and I read their books and watch their movies."

"And live in their society. And emulate them in a thousand different ways. Without us, you do not exist. It's a parasitic relationship."

"Are you calling me a parasite?"

He put up his hand. "Well, we are your food source, that much I understand."

"And not much else."

"Forgive me. I've written and memorized so many studies on you. Perhaps the terms we use in our bureaucracy are not the terms you prefer."

"I prefer Queen of Nightstalking." He stared at me. I laughed. "That was my attempt at humor."

"Please don't reject the offer out of hand."

"So you want to hire me as a hit woman for an organization that has no name. And you expect me to say yes without any sort of proof you even are who you say you are?"

"We are who we are."

"Thanks, Buddha. I'll need a bit more than that to go on."

"You'll get a car. And flights on a private jet."

"I will?" That was intriguing.

"No. I was kidding. In the bureau, they call me the joker. I'm aware that you have rules about which food you'll consume. There's obviously a moral dimension to it. I've estimated that up to twenty percent of your time is consumed—sorry not quite the right word—by your need to find morally acceptable food. Most humans in western society are only spending five percent of their time hunting and gathering their food. We could save you so much time."

It was true. I wasted so much time on research. And the truth was I was growing bored of sifting through all the details to find yet another human who had killed his wife/brother/passerby. Imagine if you had to study a specific cow for several hours before you went out to get a hamburger. Then had to do it again the next time you ate. And again. And again. "Yes. It takes time."

"And it's boring."

Was he reading my mind? "It's not scintillating." Maybe that was why Mom disappeared. She just got bored of the whole hunting and eating thing.

"That's where we come in. We could tailor a target to your rules. All you have to do is give us a description of a morally agreeable kill."

"I prefer to use the term meal."

"Meal, then. Yes, that's the perfect term. It keeps you distant from the fact that they're sentient."

"Dolphins are sentient too. Humans eat them. And whales. And elephants."

"Sorry, I wasn't judging you. Just thinking out loud." He put his hand under his chin. It gave him a bookish look. "Here's another thought. You also have an extremely nomadic existence. How many moves has it been this year? In the

34

last ten years? Set up a new nest, research your meal. Then something invariably happens—the media writes a story or there's police pursuit—and it's time to drop everything and move. Am I correct?"

He certainly liked to talk. Oddly enough, I was starting to enjoy his voice. Dermot was making sense. I had moved six times in the last year. "Moving can be onerous. But I travel light."

"Well, as one of our agents, you wouldn't have to move. Just catch a flight, go to another country, eliminate ... I mean, eat a meal ... and return. We could tack on a few days for a holiday."

"You make it sound so simple."

"Everything will be planned out for you. And since you only dine out in one manner, you'll be much cheaper than our other eliminators."

"Eliminators? That sounds so scatological." I was finding the idea of being a hit woman rather intriguing. I did like to travel, but I preferred to have a home to come back to. "What sort of documents will you give me to prove that my moral dining code has been satisfied?"

"Anything you ask for. Bios. Photographs. Video. These are bad, bad men and women we pursue. I know you are an obsessive researcher and would demand a detailed report. After all, I planned the 'Rex' project."

"You changed the files so that I would pursue your man?"

"Yes. It takes quite a bit to change official documents and make them stand out. But I was pleased by the result."

"You didn't catch me."

He shrugged. "No, but we learned so much about you."

I didn't like the confident smile he had now.

"How did you find me here?" I asked.

"Now, does a bloodhound give up his tracking methods?"

"A hound with a broken nose does."

He put up his hands. "Ah, well then, I suppose it doesn't hurt. I just checked all the North American university and college calendars for library courses. After an hour, I came across your name. New name, but you had just signed up. And you used the same initials as last time."

I was so stupid. If they were following me in Seattle they would have known I was a library student. "I'm sorry I didn't make you work harder."

He took a sip of his tea. "Oh, it was a lot of work to find you in Seattle. But once you know a target intimately, it becomes easier to find them. You learn their habits. Their needs. Their desires."

"What are my desires?"

"Simple. Blood. Once a month. And adventure, though not too much. For someone of your abilities, you're rather staid."

Staid!

"How about this?" he said. "Just do one mission to get a feel for the process. You'll excel at it; I have no doubt. Maybe even become the best in the world." He paused to let that sink in. "If you don't like it, you're free and clear to part ways with us."

I didn't know how free and clear I would be. If they could track me here, they might be able to find me anywhere. But I could go much more incognito if I had to. "And will I have the right to refuse any mission?"

He nodded. "Absolutely. There's more than one way to skin a cat."

"What a pleasant expression," I said. I drank from my teacup.

"So you do drink tea?"

"Hydration is good for the skin. Plus, it helps me fit in. And you know how important it is to fit in."

"Well, what do you think?"

I paused. There were still so many questions I could ask. How could I trust my life to an organization whose name I didn't even know? But I could leave it at any time. If he was telling the truth, that is.

Staid. He had called me *staid.*

"Let's talk money," I said.

7

Desert Sands

Dermot never came back to class. That was interesting, and perhaps a little disappointing, but not surprising. After all, he'd done his bit. I missed his scrumptious neck.

He'd never said how they'd contact me with my "mission" details, so I continued my schooling, bit by bit putting together my Master's in Library Science with a speciality in Archival Studies. Though there were classes on web systems and metadata, I had to admit I was an old-fashioned tactile girl: index cards kept my brain focused. Give me an old book and I'd be happy. Maybe vampires were naturally anti-tech. But you didn't go into library science to set the tech world on fire. It was a safe job. You kept information. You cataloged it for future generations. Because someday, that apocalypse was gonna come, and people were going to want to borrow books on building generators.

I recognized how odd it was for me to be cataloging the human experience. Humans had written a few interesting things in their hundred thousand years or so of valid consciousness, and I'd like to ensure that knowledge remained accessible. Mom said never to fall in love with my food, but she didn't say anything about falling in love with their books.

A day passed. Then another. Then a week. I wondered if ol' Dermot had been some muscled figment of my imagination. I played and replayed our conversation. And, oddly enough, I found myself sniffing every once in a while. As if ... well, as if I could smell his scent. Or I could sniff him into existence.

Next, I'd be dressing up Dermot dolls for tea parties.

With each passing day, I grew little more desperate. It was harder to concentrate on classes, and I came very close to snapping at Professor Slemay again.

A strict regimen had always kept me on target. I was a good twenty hours into researching my next meal. I decided not to do another feeding in Montréal; it was too close to home. I'd found a few promising leads, including an ex-mayor of Toronto, whom I eventually discarded because his death would cause too much of a sensation. A man in Québec City had killed his business partner. Men certainly kept me in business since they committed ninety percent of homicides. It was a bit more fun and challenging to bring them down. And they held more blood—about five and a half quarts on average compared to women's four and a half quarts. If you only ate once a month, you wanted it to be a good meal. Skinny murderesses weren't high on my consumption list.

I hadn't settled on whom I'd pursue, and I wasn't hungry enough yet. Frankly, I was bored. The idea of new meal in an exotic locale, well, sounded so perfectly scrumptious. And I didn't even have a backup meal, though there were enough Mafia members in Montréal. As I mentioned before, that could get a little messy. I'd been shot in the leg once. If you'd ever had to wrap your leg so tightly in Saran Wrap that it cut off the circulation, take the subway home, limp to your apartment, remove a bullet from your thigh and stitch it up ... well, you wouldn't want to repeat the experience.

Then, on a Wednesday morning, a brown envelope was slid under my door. It was so 1950s. My "mission" actually came in an envelope. Not a disappearing file on my iPad. Or a USB drive that would burst into flames before I could even unplug it from my MacBook. A frakkin' manila envelope.

I heard the envelope slide under my door as I was lounging in bed. In a heartbeat and a half, I was up and across the room, wearing only my negligee. I yanked open the door. Empty hallway. There was no one going down the stairs. I lived five floors up. I looked back and forth, sniffed. Not even a scent. Maybe it was the damn drone again.

I closed the door and unwound the red string to open the envelope.

Inside were round-trip airplane tickets to Dubai. The tickets were dated for the next day. And they weren't first class. I assumed that was so I wouldn't stand out. There was also a Canadian passport under the name Anna Maclean. Hmmm. Obviously, this was my new persona. The disturbing part was the passport photograph of me staring glumly ahead. They'd photographed me at some point without my knowledge.

I shook the envelope. Nothing else came out. Where was the detailed dossier that I would peruse to figure out whether or not my meal was morally consumable? This lack of information didn't bode well. I could only assume there would be details once I arrived—that everything ol' Dermot had promised would come to fruition.

I set the envelope and its contents on my table. Then I sat in my rocking chair, took a deep breath, and rocked back and forth about a thousand times.

Once my mind was clearer, I stood up and went over to the envelope. I held up the tickets. What did I have to lose? I could see Dubai. Oil, that great generator of cash, had built a few fancy buildings there. I had a return ticket, so at worst I'd lose a weekend of my life. If I didn't like the mission, I'd just cut out and go home.

If I was going that far away, I obviously needed new shoes. So I dressed, spritzed my hair, and went to the John Fluevog shoe store on Saint-Denis. *Tomber En Amour* was stenciled on the windows. As I opened the door, bells announced my arrival.

"You have that I-want-a-new-pair-of-shoes look in your eyes." The saleswoman was in her mid-twenties and she gave me such a genuine and friendly smile that even I had to smile back.

"Guilty as charged."

"Well, I am Genevieve and I'll not rest until your feet and your soul are happy. Or should I say, soles?"

It was a lame joke but delivered with a knowing wink, so I laughed. We chatted as she hunted through box after box. She was a philosophy graduate and had a yin and yang tattoo on her left shoulder. I had the odd sense that if I were ever to make friends with a human, she might be it. I was picky. About shoes. And humans. But with her clever guidance, I bought myself a nice pair of black Edwardian Hamburgers with Cuban heels. It was an odd name for a shoe; you had to wonder what the advertising department was smoking. But you didn't want to get kicked by them. Hey, a vampiress had to celebrate every once in a while.

"There will be a new line of these in the spring," Genevieve said. "Would you like a phone call reminder? It will be the only call we make. I promise you."

"I'll be waiting by the phone," I said. Then I gave her my home number, paid cash, and said goodbye to Genevieve—my new best friend—and strode out of the store.

Less than twenty-four hours later, I found myself inside an Air Canada plane at Pierre Elliott Trudeau airport, the Edwardian Hamburgers already unstrapped and on the floor. It would be an odd feeling to go through customs as a Canadian. I'd have to get my accent and my *sorries* right. If anyone asked about hockey I was a *Habs* fan. I'd learned which team to cheer for, at least. We landed in New York. After several *sorries* and a seamless customs experience, I was on my Emirates flight and starting the long journey away from the sun. And back in sight of it again.

I didn't sleep on the flight. I was tingling with anticipation. I put in my earbuds and did a little of my homework, studiously ignoring the businessman next to me who kept stealing glances at my feet. I read my Bill Bryson book. Wondered several times if Dermot would be waiting for me at the other end. Then repeated the whole cycle again. A lifetime later, the plane landed, the door was opened, and I entered an airport that was air conditioned to perfection.

Once I stepped outside, I was slapped in the face by a wrinkle-inducing heat. My skin aged twenty years in ten seconds. This was that land where skin creams went to die.

A driver was waiting for me, a Saudi Arabian man who looked as though he'd been in that spot since pre-Biblical times. He grunted and drove me in a black car to a hotel called the Arabian Courtyard.

"This is where I'm staying?" I asked.

He grunted again and gave a nod. I attempted to tip him, but he waved away the dirham notes with yet another dismissive grunt. I took my overnight bag, stepped into the iron-hot heat again, and strode through the glass doors. I was standing on a marble floor that was so clean it reflected the ceiling. The thick pillars were white and framed in gold. And a chandelier that put the word exquisite to shame hung above me. Color me impressed.

I checked in, was given a key card, and ascended to my floor in a glass elevator. My room had pristine hardwood, one white bed, a headboard in the shape of a mosque, and two Aquafina water bottles on the teak side table. At least my unnamed benefactors had not cheapened out on the hotel. Then again, for all I knew, it may have been a cheap hotel in Dubai.

An envelope waited on the writing desk. It was a heftier pack than my previous orders. I sliced open the sleeve with my fingernail, not bothering with the string—we Fangs carried our own letter openers.

Inside were several pages of paper. And another envelope. The pages had a name: Nathan Gabriel. And the outline of his life.

I had to admit, I was expecting a terrorist or some such thing—I mean, the news was telling me every day whom to be afraid of in the world. What I didn't expect was a middle-aged white guy with nondescript features and accountant glasses. But the more I read, the more I realized Mr. Gabriel was falling well within my parameters for a morally allowable meal. He was a weapons dealer. Had lived in England and Spain, then moved to Panama. He now sold a variety of arms to a variety of regimes: AK-47s, RPGs, and heavier armaments.

It did appear that ol' Gabriel hadn't personally murdered anyone. This might have been a wasted trip. Yes, the weapons he sold caused a number of deaths. But they might have been

43

for freedom fighters or a struggling democratic nation. Gabriel himself wasn't pulling the trigger. I knew I was splitting moral hairs with a quantum knife, but I had my rules.

Then I sliced open the envelope with the photographs.

They were large, high-resolution pictures. In the first shot, he was sitting at the head of a white table in a room with no windows. Three men in handcuffs were seated along one side. In front of Gabriel was a large medieval mace with spikes coming out of the ball shape. In the next picture he was holding the mace.

I won't describe the following pictures. But it was very clear he'd ended the lives of three men.

Photographs could be faked, that much I knew. These ones were dated on the back along with a short handwritten explanation that indicated this was the death of three of his dealers who had kept some of the profits for themselves.

Gabriel obviously didn't feel much regret. He was smiling in the last shot, his mace to the photographer.

There were several problems, of course. This man was not going to be an easy target. The possibility of this had crossed my mind several times on the flight over. The nameless organization that had hired me—the Dermotters, I'd named them—had difficulty getting to this man. How hard would it be for me? Gabriel would have a very complex security system. Maybe he didn't sleep in the same bed each night. And so I was risking my life for food.

And frankly, if you had to risk your life every time you had a meal, you'd think twice about where you were picking up that prime rib.

The flip side was that I needed to shake it up a bit. Life, that is.

Speaking of shaking, I shook the envelope. A final piece of paper floated out and landed in my open palm. It had a Dubai address and a time on it. Twenty minutes from now. I didn't want to look like a slob, so I took ten minutes of that time to shower. I had seen signs at the airport reminding women to "please wear respectful clothing," so I thought it best to explore my demure side. I pulled on a silk long-sleeved shirt, a cardigan, and stretchy black pants. I clad my feet in my Edwardian Hamburgers.

Going outside was like walking into an oven.

8

A Kiss Before the Killing

"You'll have to kill him immediately."

The woman who was speaking had introduced herself as Emily, and she was Asian, but her accent was British. I'd sat down at a table in an air-conditioned restaurant called Istanbul Flower, and she'd materialized beside me, stooped to give me a kiss on the forehead, then plopped herself down on the opposite chair. I'd been so shocked by the kiss that I didn't react other than to stare. "It's good to see you, sister," she said.

Sister? Before I could make a noise or say hello, she'd started into my mission.

"I need you to remember this," she whispered. She was wearing a black abaya, with a niqab lowered to show her full face. Half-moon earrings in either ear. "I've been informed that you have a good memory."

"I never forget a face. Or someone who crosses me. Or kisses me for that matter."

"Charming. Focus on my instructions. Your target is on the 108th floor of Burj Khalifa in the residential suites. You'll have to avoid his security detail." She unfolded a map of the interior of the building. I stared at it for ten seconds before she pulled it away. "I assume you have that memorized."

"Of course," I said. The truth was, I was a little sketchy about several sections.

"Good. You'll have twenty minutes while your target is alone to kill him."

"Alone? Won't his security men be there?"

"He has his daily nap at 2:15." She flashed a hint of a smile. "His guard is outside the door. You'll eliminate the target before he wakes up."

"Eliminate? I prefer to think of it as dining."

"I have no idea what you mean," she said. And by the look in her eyes, it was the truth. I guess she didn't know I was a vampire. Perhaps she'd treat me with a bit more respect if she did. "Just do your job."

"Do you have any tools for me? You know, suction cups? Explosives?"

"You provide your own tools."

"Any particular orders on what to do with the body?"

She shook her head. "Death is the only objective."

I nodded. She was about as friendly as a wolverine.

"Do you know Dermot?" I asked. The question surprised me. I kept my face straight, no sign of emotion.

"I don't know anyone, sister. I don't even know you. It's best to keep it that way."

That wasn't an answer. Her heartbeat had sped up slightly at the mention of his name. A crush? "I see." I decided there was no point in pressing her further. She checked her iPhone, perhaps updating her Facebook status with *Orders Given*, then she stood up. "Well, sister, it's time for me to go. And you ... well, time for you to go too."

47

"Goodbye, sister," I said.

She went. It was the third longest conversation I'd had in a year. Dermot. Genevieve at the shoe store. And now Miss Secret Agent.

I took a cab to the base of Burj Khalifa. Did I mention the heat? I would need a bucket of lip gloss.

Since the dawn of mankind, men had been building homages to their penises. There was, of course, that multi-erectile construction called Stonehenge and also the leaning tower of Pisa. I was sure many could comment on the symbolism. And finally, most "size-matters" of all, there was Burj Khalifa.

Burj Khalifa was arguably one of the most impressive buildings on earth. Strike that—it was *the* most impressive. A giant, segmented erection, although it was usually more politely described as a finger that disappeared into the heavens. Standing at the bottom, I couldn't bend my neck far enough to see the top. There was a bit of cloud up there.

The tower offered a rich array of amenities and services that provided residents and their guests an unparalleled lifestyle experience. I'd gotten that info from the brochure. I didn't really care.

Gaining entry to the hotel was not so hard, since tourists were allowed inside. In fact, they clogged up the sidewalk, the grounds, and the lobby. I pushed my way past the gawkers and bought a ticket to the observation deck.

The glass elevator rose forever toward the heavens.

I did feign being unimpressed by what human beings had created in this world. The Louvre was marvelous. And the city of New York was a jewel. But I'd never been stunned speechless by anything human-made. I must admit I stood agog as I came to the observation deck and looked out. The city spread out before me like a collection of jewels. Beyond that was desert. And distance. The curve of the earth appeared to be visible. It was perhaps the most beautiful view I'd had during my short time on this earth.

I took a moment to stare, then went off to kill a weapons dealer.

9

Old School

I went old school.

By that, I mean I waited until the crowds had thinned, snuck into the women's washroom, hung my cardigan on a hook, and climbed up a vent. Yes, it could be that simple. It was a moment's work to remove the vent cover, another moment to pop up there and begin crawling along. The metal sheeting didn't even creak. I crawled left and right, following the map inside my head. I could be clever sometimes. My mom used to tell me so.

Which made the getting lost part rather frustrating. I found myself in a vast spider web of vents that doubled back on each other. I thought I might get stuck in a cul-de-sac forever, and they'd find my double-jointed bones a thousand years from now when the tower finally fell. I came across one vent that dropped straight down. I couldn't see the bottom.

Never fall prey to your own cleverness. Mom also liked to say that. You know, she really could have put together a tidy little self-help book.

Eventually, I had to admit my failure, and I quietly undid a vent cover and popped my head out. A rotund woman, who had perhaps had more candy than she needed, was bathing below me, eyes closed. If she opened them at that moment, she would've been looking directly up at me. I glanced out the window and got my bearings then pulled the lid back on and continued along what I hoped was the right path.

I checked my phone. Three minutes until nap time for old Mr. Gabriel. I hit another dead end, then mistakenly crawled into a vent that got smaller and smaller. I backed out and skittered down another artery. It was extremely hard to hurry through a vent system.

I checked the time. Gabriel was well into his nap. Counting dead sheep, likely.

I was somewhat certain I was above his compartment. I listened, but there wasn't a sound, and I couldn't see through the tin. I undid the screws with my nails. Popped my head out—right beside a security camera. Below me, asleep on the bed, was Mr. Gabriel. A pillow propped up his knees. So he really did nap every day. And, if he was on schedule, he'd been asleep for over fifteen minutes. I'd read that naps were healthy for you. I've never had time myself.

His nap was about to become endless. I cut the wires to the camera—there were likely others stationed about the room. And who knew what security tricks he had up his sleeve? I took thirty seconds to scout the room. I had four and a half minutes before his guard would return.

I hated being late for a meal. And I hated rushing to finish it.

I dropped down to the floor, landing quietly. So far, so good. No alarms had gone off. No infrared beams cut across the room; I would have seen them. Maybe he was more into brute force. The guard at the door was enough to ward away most would-be enemies. And really, who'd be able to climb to these heights other than me? I stretched, and one of my vertebrae cracked, but Mr. Joseph did not slide open a curious eye. I took in a Zen breath.

He let out the slightest snore. He was a well-muscled specimen. He hadn't put on any fat since the photographs had been taken. He had laid out his suit jacket on the chair and there were underarm sweat stains on his shirt. A Luger sat on his bed table; no surprise since he was likely a collector, and I fully expected the thing to be in perfect firing shape. Maybe he had a thing for Nazis too.

Well, this was it. It did take a bit of time to suck out the blood. And I'd be sluggish afterward. I wasn't looking forward to dragging my heavy body back through the vent system. Seven to eight percent of body weight is blood. And judging by Gabriel's size, I'd be putting on about twelve pounds—tough on a girl's figure. That was why I owned stretch pants.

I crawled across the bed, paused a microsecond to admire a gold skull button protector on his top button, then dipped down to sink my teeth into his jugular.

The moment my teeth touched his neck, a shock shot through me, strong enough to throw me from the bed. I rolled across the floor. My lips were actually burning. I wiped them with a jittery hand.

The skull button had been a personal electroshock device with some kind of sensor inside it.

Gabriel opened his eyes. There was a trickle of blood on his neck. He sat up and reached for his Luger. I knocked it from the bedside table—well, I knocked over the table too. Bad aim. I still couldn't quite stand. My muscles were jerking.

"Well," he said. "I guess the conducted electrical button works. One can never be too cautious."

Electricity was not my friend. But I got my wits back much faster than most.

"Obviously," I said. Which was the cleverest thing I could come up with. Again, I was in the odious position of having to talk to my food. It was just so wrong and depressing. All I wanted was a quiet meal and a glass of wine.

"May I ask who you are?" he said.

"There isn't a lot of time," I answered. "I have to kill you then go shopping."

"I assume you're not the bed turning service." He eyed the open vent. "Ah, I see. A spider."

I leapt, but he was off the bed before I could get to him. This was the second human who could move faster than should be possible.

"We aren't done talking," he said. "I want to know who you are before I cut off your pretty little head."

"I'm your fairy godmother." I really had to work on my repartee. But, as I said before, I usually didn't talk before I ate. And my nerves were still buzzing with electricity. Fifty thousand volts took several seconds to shake off.

He lifted a yellow Taser gun from his opposite bedside table. "These seem to work on you." He fired it.

I couldn't dodge a bullet most of the time, but the Taser fired electrode projectiles that weren't quite as speedy. I dodged the bolts, hearing them hiss as they shot by. The wires that followed to deliver the shock landed uselessly on the floor. "Oh, you're quick," he said. "Impressive."

His confidence was a little unnerving. But I must admit, my ire was up. And the taste of his blood tingled on my lips. I needed more. More! I made a feint one way and smashed a left hook into his jaw. That knocked a bit of the confidence out of

53

him, but he'd moved fast enough to make it a glancing blow.

He jumped back off the bed and was now framed against the window, the whole big city of Dubai behind him. "Who sent you?" he asked.

"The ghosts of all those people you killed," I said. Okay, I admit that was a little too melodramatic.

The door opened behind me and his guard walked in. "Boss?" he said. I delivered a back kick that connected with the guard's temple, and he crumpled to the floor. One of my expensive Edwardian Hamburgers flew off. I nearly screamed in rage. The shoes had two belts and a zipper so that should never have happened, but it was proof of how hard I kicked the man. The heels were a good inch long. Which made me lopsided. I sliced my nails through the straps and kicked off the second shoe. I'd be charging that to the Dermotters. I fought better on my bare feet anyway.

"Well, that's also impressive," Mr. Gabriel said. I'm not certain whether or not he was referring to the shoes or my quick strike on his bodyguard.

He pulled a wicked-looking knife from his belt. But that gave me heart. He was down to the most basic of weapons. "I wonder how much you cost?" he asked. And yes, he did stroke the knife blade and leer as he asked. A walking, meat-eating cliché.

"I can be bought for a meal."

He touched his neck. "Hmmm," he said. "I thought you were trying to cut my throat. But now that I think of it, I don't see a knife. And there's blood on your lips. My blood."

He was putting far too much together, far too quickly. I guess you didn't get to the top of the weapons heap by being dull-witted.

I took a step toward him. He assumed a fighting stance.

"I did try to hire one of you only a short while ago," he said.

"One of me?" I said.

"Yes. A *homo sapiens vampiris.*"

"We are not on your family tree!"

"One does not argue with science. But I'll stick with vampire. A blood-sucking fiend."

"Fiend? How crass."

As I said before, I found his calmness unnerving. I wasn't used to humans knowing that I, or my kind, really existed. In fact, I preferred we be left off the species chart altogether. "And where did you come up with this mad idea?"

He flashed the knife. "I know a lot about your kind now, actually. You need to feed once a month. You go mad when you don't, especially when you're chained. Your reflexes are faster than humans by about twenty-five percent."

"I assume you didn't learn this in grade school."

"No, a complicated series of tests. A shame our subject died."

I couldn't help it. I pictured my mother shackled to a chair in some desert bunker. Going mad from the lack of blood.

"Who did you experiment on?"

"Oh, he didn't have a name. Not one that we could trust anyway."

He? I didn't know any *he* vampires. Well, there was that shadowy, nameless figure known as my father. The fact Gabriel had captured one of my kind was not good news.

I'd discerned how fast he really was from how quickly he'd escaped from the bed and nearly avoided my blow. The knife likely wouldn't kill me. But I didn't want a hole in my nice shirt. Or my ribcage.

"How do you know that my kind haven't sent me as revenge?"

I said.

"Ha. They're disorganized. Scattered across the world. Most of you don't even do much more than scramble from meal to meal. Not the smartest of species."

We were the top of the food chain. We didn't scramble.

So I decided to end it. "You're so nine hundred," I said.

This confused him. And well it should have—it's an old librarian joke. You see, nine hundred is where we file the history books under the Dewey Decimal System. So I was saying, "You're history." It kills at librarian parties.

Not so much in this situation.

Anyway, he continued to look a little confused. So I charged him. Skinny and svelte ol' me against a two hundred fifty-pound barbarian blood-pumping machine.

He was going to taste oh so good.

10

Turns Out, I Bleed

I'd like to tell you it was easy. That with a flick of my wrist, I knocked him out and sucked all the blood from his body. But the bastard could move.

He darted out of the way, flashed in with the knife, and sliced my shirt and my shoulder. The cut was deep enough to make a rivulet of red run down my arm. Now I knew why the ninjas wore black—to hide their wounds. The sight of blood brought a leer to his face.

"And yes, I know you bleed too," he said. "We experimented with that. Though we didn't wait to see if your kind could bleed to death."

Oh, how I wanted to take his head off his shoulders. He'd tortured one of my brethren. And he didn't feel any remorse for that. The reasons to kill him were piling up.

"You move quickly," I said. It was as close to a compliment as I'd give him.

"I may have been augmented." He flexed his arm muscles and made his chest muscles dance like some beach bum weightlifter. "We studied your kind. Very closely. We were able to do a gene subtraction here, a gene injection there. It does come in rather handy. Makes the teeth whiter too."

He flicked the knife again and caught my left arm. This time there was an actual gash. It hurt, and not just my pride. My arm was burning, and I was very aware of how quickly the blood was coming out of me. I'll be honest. I was not used to being cut. Or taunted. I preferred the takedown to be over in a few seconds. But my heart was beating faster, my breathing was shallower, and panic was flapping its wings at the edge of my thoughts. All the signs that I'd become the prey.

"You men," I said, forcing myself not to look at the wound. "You always feel the need to get things augmented. Never take the time to work on your personalities."

I thought it was clever. He laughed. Well, growled was more like it.

"I'll enjoy doing experiments on you," he said. Yes, he actually said that.

He was growing more confident with each second. And well he should have, since I was the only one doing any heavy bleeding. But maybe he was overconfident. He slashed out, and I raked my claws across his chest, four marks that spouted blood. Enough to make his white shirt red and dull the egotistical sheen in his eyes.

"I prefer my food not to get overly excited before a meal," I said.

Then I dodged another blow and stepped up to him, nails aiming for his throat. But he was a street fighter and smashed his forehead into mine. I caught his arm and, with a move Mom taught me, used his momentum to launch him against one of the floor-to-ceiling windows.

Now, normally it would take a tank to drive through the glass on these modern buildings. But with his weight and my

58

speed and the thickness of his head—well, he actually made a satisfying spider web of cracks. So I slammed him up against it again and again. Adrenaline was overriding the logic center of my brain. Smack! Smack! Smack! Then the window broke behind him. It was not the type of glass that would shatter, but it did come loose from the windowsill and fall backward. I failed to notice this, and the last slam of his head met with open air. He slipped out of my grip. I grabbed his shoulder, slowing his fall enough that he was able to catch the edge with his fingertips.

I hefted him partway up. "You won't let me fall," he said. "You want to know what I know." It was windy, and I could easily be pulled down with him. And I wouldn't turn into a bat on the way down. So I dug the nails of my right hand into the plush carpet. Dug my feet in too and lifted him up about eight more inches, grunting in an unladylike fashion.

"It may be that the female of the vampire species is faster and stronger than the male," I said. "Maybe you didn't get to test that."

Then I began to feed.

"Wait!" he shouted. "Waaaiiit!" He struggled for a moment, but the paralytic agent in my fangs made him sluggish, and he began his second nap of the day. He was dead a minute later.

"That's for wrecking my shoes."

I dropped him. His body did a couple of twists and turns and a pirouette through the air. He hit terminal velocity and would soon hit something else. No sense watching the messy part.

I wiped my mouth and straightened my clothing. I took a moment to glance in his mirror. I looked like hell heated up in a microwave. And I had gained several pounds.

I squished my bloated body through the vent, closed it quietly, and crawled back the way I'd come. A few floors below, I lowered myself into the bathroom of an empty apartment. My wounds were already closing. Another nice trick of my body—I healed fast. They itched with pain, and I did still feel tight in the chest as if I might never catch my breath. But I was alive. And he was dead. His blood gurgled in my belly. I opened the front door and went to the elevator.

I left Burj Khalifa in bare feet.

11

Roses Have Thorns

I slept very deeply. The next morning, my skin was so dry it was flaking. The same grumpy driver took me back to the airport. There always was the chance that some camera had caught the feeding. So as I waited in the airport, I kept one eye on a flat-screen TV. There were Al Jazeera reports about a man who, through a freak accident, had fallen to his death from Burj Khalifa. The theory was that a drone had flown into the window, weakening it, and he had leaned on the glass. Al Jazeera played a short and not very illuminating bio of Gabriel. He was labeled as an investment manager in the military industry.

There obviously wasn't any cameras that recorded the battle, or I would've been caught. Or else the cameras belonged to Gabriel.

It dawned on me that I hadn't bought a keepsake, so I went to one of those keepsake stands and picked out a ring in the shape of a snake. Its eyes were jade, and it fit perfectly on my little finger. My one memento.

I slept most of the way home, despite being so close to so many humans. A full stomach did that. I struggled to open my eyes once we'd landed in New York, then I stumbled to my flight to Montréal. A few hours later, I blink-walked my way to a cab and was soon back in my apartment. Dubai was far, far behind me. Though I still had sand in my eyes.

By Monday afternoon, I was sitting in my *History of Books and Printing* class and learning about the history of the printing press. Over the next week, my life returned to normal. While Dubai had been exotic and exciting, I didn't want to become an adrenaline junkie. That'd be the end of me. Mom had warned me about that.

I did wonder if I'd dined on Gabriel a little too soon. I could have learned more about my species. But when you had to fight your food, you tended to want to eat it quickly. I had learned there were others like me. This, of course, I already knew or had at least been told by my mother and DBI (Dermot's Bureau of Intelligence). But Gabriel had been based in Panama, and there'd been a vampire there.

There couldn't be too many of us around. If thirty were in the United States, that might not get noticed. Only an extra three hundred sixty deaths a year didn't make a dent in the statistics, as long as we covered our tracks. Severely exsanguinated corpses would become a story at coroners' conventions. But three hundred vampires feeding twelve times a year? That's three thousand six hundred corpses. We were getting into rather large numbers that authorities might notice. No, it was obvious that we were a very small nation. Or we spent a lot of time in those backward countries.

But we existed. I was proof. So was my mother. And now there was Gabriel's tale of experimenting on a vampire. I was not enthused about the idea that we were being examined by such unscrupulous characters and that those experiments had resulted in augmented—What? Muscles? Reflexes?—so that

Gabriel could almost match my speed.

I wasn't certain I wanted another assignment like that.

Anyway, at about 3:00 p.m. on the Thursday after my return, there was a *knock knock knock* at my door.

I was a naturally paranoid individual. It was a survival mechanism that Mom instilled in me since birth. *Never trust anyone but me.* It did tend to stick. I doubted I could be traced to Gabriel's death, but he obviously came from a large network, and they may have had methods I couldn't imagine. I didn't want to end up in one of their chimpanzee cages.

Anyway, I couldn't sit there until I got all moldy. But I didn't want to look through the peephole. It was a good way to get shot. So I went out onto my balcony and crawled about three feet across the old stucco siding, digging my nails in far enough to leave indentations. Stucco was falling to the ground as I peeked through the hallway window. Dermot was standing at my door, rubbing his chin with one hand and holding flowers wrapped in brown paper in the other. Of all the things in the world, I did not expect flowers. My heart fluttered momentarily until I stomped those feelings to pieces. Had I read "Cinderella" too many times?

I jumped down onto my balcony, hopped to my door, opened it, grabbed the flowers, and, just as he was opening his lips to say something, slammed the door. Capricious, that was my middle name. I enjoyed his shocked expression. Well, what I saw of it.

I went into my mini-kitchen and began digging through the cupboard for a vase. He opened the door a moment later. "Oh do come in," I said as I slit the waxy paper open with my fingernail. Twelve perfectly formed roses. "Very kind of you to bring these for little ol' me. Does everyone get them after a

63

mission?"

"Only the good agents," he said without any hint of sarcasm. "I would've brought champagne. But I know you don't drink alcohol."

"I do when I'm in the mood for it," I said. I sliced off the stems with my fingernails and a few seconds later had them in a vase with water. I took a deep breath through my nostrils. Having heightened senses meant that smells were amplified, and the roses gave off a scent that was heavenly and calming.

I was touched. Perhaps I did have an iota of romance in my heart. No one had brought me roses before. No one had dared. It was kind of hard to date when your mom was always hovering over your shoulder shouting, *Eat the boys, don't date them!*

"You did an excellent job, according to reports," Dermot said. "Well, perhaps a little dramatically for our tastes."

"The target was a tiny bit tougher than I'd anticipated."

"His body disappeared," he said.

"Into thin air? Or do you mean into lots of little pieces?"

"Yes, falling from that height wasn't that good for the structural integrity of his corpse."

"That's a clever way to say he was smashed like a rotten pumpkin."

"I'm a clever guy." He tapped his skull with a thick index finger. "Though perhaps it was you who was being the cleverest, because dropping him from such a height meant that no one would notice he was missing most of his blood. Might even have erased any of the feeding marks."

"Yes, I am that clever," I said, though really, I'd been desperate. And that lull that came after feeding was what had made me loosen my grip. His falling body could've accidentally killed some innocent tourists far below, now that I thought of it. That would have broken one of Mom's holy rules.

"His remains were scraped up and taken to the coroner," Dermot continued. "Then they did, indeed, disappear."

"I guess his comrades needed to do their own study on why he died."

"That's our assumption. What was he like?"

"Unseemly. Egotistical. And he used too much aftershave."

"And you had difficulty subduing him?"

I shrugged. "There was a battle royale, so to speak. Maybe fifty or so seconds long. Much longer than I'm used to. And I lost a pair of shoes, which I'll be charging you for. Oh, and he said he was augmented. I don't understand the science myself, just being a simple librarian. But he was stronger. Faster. All those things you males seem to like. Maybe even faster than you. He had a few gene splices from a vampire."

"He had encountered vampires?"

I must say I was relishing having information that ol' Dermot didn't seem to know. "Apparently he'd captured a male, studied him, and killed him." It could have been my father. I tightened my grip on one of the roses, and its head snapped off. I set it on the counter. "It makes me wonder who else has been augmented with vampire genes. Someone I may know."

"Me?" he laughed. "Not that way. Vitamins. And the good old-fashioned way. "

"Which is what?"

"Scientific experiments. Adjustments here and there. And I work out. A lot." He seemed to beam pride, and I swear his chest stuck out another inch or so.

"I know," I said. I wriggled my nose.

"But I've showered. You—"

"—have a delicate sense of smell. Anyway, about this line of

65

work. I'm not certain I want to do it anymore."

"Why?" he asked.

"Because I'm risking my life for a meal. Normally, I don't risk my life. This was fun for a lark. But maybe I'll only accept easily consumed food from your ... food services organization."

"The whole point of our approaching you and creating this agreement is that these are difficult targets."

"You sound like a lawyer."

"I'm trained in law. I'm trained in many things."

I lifted one of the roses. "Then you will understand that every contract can be given an addendum. I need a better payoff. I can get food anywhere. It's all around me, as you see."

He was watching me closely.

"What do you want, Amber Fang?"

The way he said my name threw me. Only my mother and he had said my real name aloud. I drew in my breath. "Well, Dermot, I want your knowledge. About my kind. About why this arms dealer had, as far as I know, his very own vampire to experiment on. And how many vampires are out there."

Dermot smiled a handsome smile. "Ah, what if we don't have any knowledge that is of interest to you?"

"Well, I could work for someone else." A naked lie. I didn't know anyone else. He knew that too. "I'd have to join LinkedIn."

"Well, well," he said. "I wouldn't want you to lower yourself to that. I'll admit to not being very much in the know myself. I'll talk to my higher-ups."

"You do that." I felt pretty confident in my position. I had just proved how effective I could be. They would not have any other hired guns like me. Or hired teeth, I should say. "And ..." An emotion swept over me. "And I want you to find my mother." This had come out of the blue. But once the idea shot out my mouth, I seized on it. "Yes, that's it. And my father too," I added.

His eyes darkened. "That's not an easy thing to do."

"You found me," I said. "Mom—she has to be out there somewhere, right? And I'd like to see my father once. I want to look in his eyes. I just ..." Ah, this was sounding sappy. "I just want to see him."

"I honestly don't know if that's within the realm of possibility."

"Bring it within the realm of possibility. I thought you had a big organization. You tracked me down. Those same methods should work for them."

"But you were sloppy."

"I was not!"

He shrugged as if there was no point in arguing. "I'm just saying that we've spent decades hunting. And we have captured ... I mean, contacted very few of your kind."

"So you've contacted other vampires?"

"Not successfully."

File that under vague response.

"So you killed one of my species?" I asked.

"We've had encounters, that's all. We lost some good men."

We'd have to leave it vague.

"Well, those are the terms of my deal. Find my mother and my father and give me more of your vague information. Take it or leave it."

"I'll see what I can do," he said carefully. "Enjoy your flowers."

Then he turned and walked out of my apartment. His scent remained. It wasn't as unpleasant as I'd let on.

67

12

A Cheap Envelope

I rotated back into my usual routine. Mom's voice began to shout, *You've been here too long, it's safer to move! Go. Go. Go.* Hey, her voice had kept me alive for a long time. But I ignored it. I was sick of pulling up stakes (and be careful how you use that word around vampires) every time I got a strange whiff.

I needed to find my main meal for this month, and an easy backup meal. A week passed. Then another. I tapped my fingers several times.

I read *The Montréal Gazette.* I was beginning to understand the citizens of Québec lived and breathed their politics. The *French versus English versus French versus everyone* debate continued unabated. Bridges were falling apart, and there was a sugges-tion mobsters were somehow involved with the construction contracts. Oh, these humans and their trivial concerns. But you never knew what you'd find in a paper. Sometimes even your next meal will pop out of the pages.

When I was flipping through the back pages, I came across a familiar face. A woman had been stabbed to death in a robbery. There were the usual *police are not commenting* and guesswork by the reporter. Normally, I'd skip this sort of stuff, but I'd seen the woman before. It was Genevieve, the saleswoman from the Fluevog shoe store. She'd been vivacious. Fun. And someone had killed her for whatever money was in the till. The murderer or murderers had arrived at closing and spray painted over the security camera. I could only imagine Genevieve's fear and pain.

I sliced out the article with my fingernail. I'd find that killer. See if he had any remorse. And if not, I'd give him something to be remorseful about. In the few seconds it took me to feed, that is. Yes, I liked that idea. It would be worth the risk to eat a little closer to home. *Never kill the woman who sells me my shoes.* I'd write it on the guy's forehead.

Of course, I assumed the perp was male. That's how the percentages went.

My heartbeat sped up, followed by a rush of adrenaline.

As I put the article on the table, I was surprised by a bout of sadness. I'd spent maybe thirty minutes with Genevieve, but she'd had *joie de vivre* to the max. And now that *joie* was dead. I nearly shed a tear.

Why was I so concerned about food? I had to put my anger on the backburner. No sense jumping into something while you were emotional. And I wasn't a detective. It's not like I could go around interviewing people. The gendarmes would have to hunt for the killer first.

But even behind bars, he wouldn't be safe.

The third week after my return from Dubai, another envelope slid under my door. I didn't open the door this time, though I was still curious as to who or what was dropping the envelopes off. I sliced it open, noticing it wasn't the highest quality stationary. Unimpressive.

There was one piece of paper inside. I slid it out and read:

All agreements with Amber Fang are herewith terminated.

That was it. Not even a signature. I smelled the envelope. But there wasn't a scent either. As if no human hands had touched it. Maybe it had been written by robots.

I leapt to the door and yanked it open. Sniffed. No scent. No sign of who or what had dropped it off. I slammed the door and sat on the end of my bed.

I bit my lip. Hard. This didn't seem to be a negotiating tactic. Normally you didn't play hardball right after the first offer. And if the agreements were terminated, what did that mean? Would they take me away to one of those interrogation pens? Remove my vital organs?

They wouldn't leave me alone. Not now that they knew who I was. Where I was. I was sure they wished there was a way to take my set of skills and use them for their own purposes. And if Mom's *flee* voice was whispering before, it was shouting now. *Run! Run! Run!Back to Mommy.* Okay, I added that last bit in.

I crumpled the paper up. They had rejected the most efficient killer they could have had. The humans had turned me down. And Dermot couldn't even do it face-to-face. He had chosen to dump me with a piece of paper. The bastard! And it wasn't even nice paper. Double bastard!

The roses were on the floor and the vase smashed before my heart had beat another beat. I looked around for something else that reminded me of them. Of Dermot.

There was nothing. Nothing! But I wanted—no needed—to break more things. Bones perhaps. Noses. Punch through walls and scare the bejeepers out of my neighbors. That'd teach them to have loud late-night sex romps.

How could food reject me?

Hell hath no fury like a vampiress scorned.

70

I sat in the corner, and for the first time in a very long time, I actually felt as if I might cry. I hadn't cried since my mother had left. Not once.

"Go to hell," I whispered. "All of you humans can go to hell."

No tears slipped down my cheek. But the very idea that they were on the edge of my eyelids made my anger rise. So much so, I imagined the tears burning up before they could form.

No one rejected me. I'd formed attachments and been swindled. My ego had been rubbed, and I'd responded like a puppy dog. This was not the Fang way.

I stormed out of the apartment.

I walked. I strode and stomped. Up the Mont Royal mountain of Montréal to the chalet. It takes a few hours to get to the top. Unless you're particularly mad and willing to charge up the road double time. I looked down on the city, and all the lights gathered there. Full of brightness and people. It was a particularly attractive city. And perhaps somewhere in that city was Dermot.

Was he sleeping comfortably in a soft bed tonight? Already thinking about the next agent he would seduce with words and tickets to exotic locations? Could he just walk away from me like that?

I seethed. I cursed. I tightened my fists and shook them at the city.

Uselessly, of course. But it made me feel a bit better. I would've let out a scream if I had thought it would have helped.

I decided I'd find him. I'd find *them*. And they would answer my questions. It would be time for a new deal. Once I had a plan of action, or even a germ of a plan, I'd put all my energies toward it.

I tried to mentally grasp how huge my task would be. This

was a secret organization. It's not like they left their address anywhere. Montana? Moscow? I couldn't even state what their purposes truly were. And they had enough money for drones, chemical research, and to send me (and how many other agents) around the world to kill bad guys.

Ah, but I was a librarian-in-training, and my brain was a highly developed research tool. Whether there was any sort of paper trail, I couldn't be certain. Where would I start? It would all come to me, I decided. Oh, those little boys in their suits would probably dirty their Superman shorts when I dropped out of an air vent and said, "Hello, it's time to talk. Let's begin by tearing out your throats."

That made me smile. Revenge was a dish best served in a shocking manner.

They had more answers than I did about my own kind. And there would be a way to make them give me that information. Or to renegotiate the deal we'd had. That was my intention. To obtain a stronger, fairer deal.

My confidence had risen like the phoenix, and the walk back down the mountain of Montréal was more of a pleasant jog. Even the little bit of rain and chill didn't dampen my feelings. I had a new purpose. I wouldn't have been surprised if I'd looked back and seen my footprints on fire.

After several minutes, I was making my way to Saint-Denis street. A fire truck passed me, lights flashing and siren doing its best banshee impression. With the *Service desécurité incendie deMontréal* symbol on the door. I liked fire trucks. There was something about those massive red trucks and all those firefighters, rich with blood. A pretty common sight in Montréal. This one was followed by a police car. *Service de Police de la Ville de Montréal—SPVM*. Gendarmes. This, in turn, was followed by an ambulance.

This was a big city. Things happened. Crime. Car crashes. Fire. People died. Not a night went by without sirens waking me up. I was a light sleeper. Sometimes I'd howl along with them.

I was kidding about that last part. I was not a werewolf. There were no werewolves. I know. I'd looked.

When I turned down my block and saw that the emergency vehicles were collecting at my apartment building and that it was on fire, I broke into a run.

A crowd had gathered, despite the drizzle. I'd speculated the old structure would fall down on its own in the next decade or so. Apparently, if it got smacked by a bomb, it collapsed rather quickly.

The window of my apartment was a gaping hole, and the inside was all flames. The whole building sagged below that point, looking like it was frowning.

There had obviously been an attempt to permanently terminate my contract.

13

A Familiar Scent

The only things I'd miss was the picture I had of Mom and some of my favorite clothes. New clothes could be bought, but the picture couldn't be replaced. I still had one in my wallet of dear old Nigella. That was Mom's name by the way. Yes, it was a stupid name for a vampire. Nigella Fang. That didn't exactly inspire fear. But she was born a hundred years ago, and they liked different names back then.

I watched the firemen fight the flames with a giant hose and didn't even have the presence of mind to make a phallic joke. I was obviously still in shock. It slowly dawned on me that someone had tried to take my life. My muscles already knew—I was shaking.

The assassination attempt hadn't been very efficient. They hadn't even checked to see if I was home and didn't seem to care that they were risking the lives of all the other tenants too.

Whoever had done it might have even been watching the spectators for me. I pulled my hood up. Every face I saw was suspicious, though all of them were gawking at the flames.

The crowd was getting larger and larger, police trying to shoo them back with a bull horn: "*Arrêtez! Arrêtez! Retourner à vos résidences!*" Officers were efficiently setting up a yellow police tape perimeter.

They tried to kill me. They actually tried to kill me.

I hadn't quite determined who *they* were yet. I doubted it would be revenge for Gabriel's death. They'd have no idea where I lived. This seemed more like a clumsy attempt by Dermot.

My hands were fists. And there was a cop coming toward me telling me to, "*Reculez! Reculez!*" I nearly punched him. But I backed up and slid between a mom with a lit cigarette in her mouth, her toddler hanging off her shoulder, and an old lady leaning on a walker. The flames were growing higher. Clearly, the blast had gone inward, not outward as it would in a gas explosion. That made me wonder if it was some sort of rocket. I was not particularly knowledgeable about ordnance blast patterns.

The bastards tried to kill me.

Anger wasn't a great place to start from when you were in need of logic. But what was very clear to me was my days in Montréal and Canada were done. It was time to retreat. To forge a new identity, just as Mom had taught me, and work my way south, perhaps to Mexico, along all the back highways to avoid an organized hunt. I didn't want to take any American flights because Dermot and his pals likely had some sort of connection with Homeland Security. A flight from Canada to Europe might be possible. I was good at travelling light.

The logical thing to do was to leave right away.

I'll kill every last one of them.

I was clearly getting into revenge territory, which went against my moral code and, frankly, was not good for keeping a low profile. *Don't get emotional, Dear,* Mom had always said. But she'd never had an explosive shot into her home.

I need you, Mom. I need you now.

I caught a familiar scent. Only a few disparate molecules were floating through the air, mixed with the smoke, the sweat of the crowd, and the mothball scent coming off the old lady. But those few molecules sent my senses tingling, and I bared my teeth.

Dermot's stink. Yes, he'd been near this spot. When I looked at what I guessed was the angle of entry to launch a rocket, I was in the perfect place to stand.

Coincidence? I think not.

I sniffed loudly and with such vigor that the single mom beside me looked over.

"I've got a cold," I said.

She nodded, clutching her sleeping toddler. *Put your kid to bed,* I wanted to say.

But in that inhalation, I found a few more particles of ol' Dermot. And I sniffed again. Nudging my way to the left, then right through the crowd. Each moment, his scent grew a little stronger. The traitor had actually tried to kill me. After all that talk. The long inane conversation. The flowers. The compliments he'd given me about my ability to kill.

Well, he'd see that first hand.

I followed my nose. Literally. Sniffing here and there, getting a few odd looks from the humans around me. His scent grew fresher as I worked my way along the street then turned down an alley. He'd run this way; I could tell by the way his particles were spread out. He had paused and leaned against a brick wall. His hands were wet. I actually found a palm print. The bastard had been there not five minutes ago. He'd dropped sweat on the ground too.

With each step, I was getting closer. He must have spent a good thirty seconds in that location to leave all of those pheromones.

Then he went down another alley. I was no more than two minutes behind him judging by the distribution of particles. The alley opened up onto the eternally busy *Avenue Van Horne*. His scent was so strong, I expected to bump into him any second. I pulled my hood up tighter and sniffed.

His scent stopped on the edge of the sidewalk between two parked cars. Cabs of all colors were going by. A city bus *squuuueaashed* its brakes.

He had hailed a cab. And was gone. Not less than forty-five seconds earlier. If it was on this side of the street, he was heading west. Traffic was slow because of the "accident." The police had likely already set up checkpoints.

So I ran down the street to where the cars were stopped for a red light. I kept low and glanced through the windows of the cars, dodging pedestrians who were coming home from work. I looked at the occupants of each cab I passed: frumpy old man, a businessman, an old woman clutching her groceries.

Then the familiar back of a head with short, curly hair. He had his face in his hands. I skidded to a stop and backed up. Soon, I would have his head in my hands.

I cut between the parked cars and briefly toyed with the idea of smashing through the window and poking out his eyes. Instead, with a burst of adrenaline, I sank my nails into the door and pulled it off the cab. Vampire strength comes in handy when you wanted to, well, take a door off a cab.

I grabbed him by the front of his long jacket and yanked him out of the car. Lucky for him, he hadn't fastened his seatbelt, or I might have torn him in half.

He smashed into a red VW, and for a moment, I thought I'd killed him. Then he got to his feet.

"Amber," he said. His eyes were red.

"Yes, surprise, surprise, I'm not dead." I smacked him in the head.

Normally that would have killed someone. I must've held back because he rubbed his face and stood up.

Then I came for him, nails out. He caught my hand and with a Jiu-Jitsu-type move, tossed me into the side of a blue city bus. It was a nice flip. And it hurt like hell.

"Stop it," he said.

"But we've only started!" I flipped back onto my feet and charged toward him. He stood still for a moment then turned and began to flee.

Ah, there was nothing more exhilarating than chasing prey.

I pursued.

14

Stand Down

The bastard could run.

But I gained on him. He turned to ward me off, so I shoved him through a shop window. Male mannequins went flying, arms and limbs scattering as if a grenade had gone off.

"Stop it!" he said. "Stand down!"

I swung. He caught my hand. I swung with the other. And he caught it. "Just stop fighting and listen."

The words were an invitation to do more damage. I twisted up and kicked him in the chin. He fell back, knocking over another mannequin. An alarm was *ring-ding-dinging* madly.

I leapt on him, held his shoulders down with my knees, and clamped my left hand around his neck. I was so tempted to just pull out his esophagus. He was breathing hard.

He looked as if he'd been crying. Weakling. I almost slapped him.

I released my pressure.

"Speak," I said. "Why were you trying to kill me?"

He blinked. "I wasn't. I didn't."

"Don't lie! You were there. You fired the rocket launcher at my apartment."

"I'm certain it was a rocket propelled grenade. I arrived a few minutes after your apartment was hit."

"Yeah, right."

"I've been keeping my eye on you."

I squeezed a little tighter. "I bet you have. To terminate the contract forever?"

"I told you, I didn't fire the RPG."

"Then which one of your henchmen did it?"

"None of us. We don't work that way. We never kill innocent bystanders."

I was tempted to stick my fingers in his ears and make them meet in the middle. "Why should I believe a backstabber?"

"Amber." It was still odd to hear him say my name. "We wouldn't have been this messy. We're not an organization that draws attention to itself. At all. We would've chosen a much quieter death for you. This smacks of ... well ... of heavy-handedness."

"What heavy-handed thugs want to kill me?" I asked. It was becoming clear that I had perhaps—just perhaps—jumped to the wrong conclusion.

"It's not a coincidence this occurred so soon after your trip to Dubai."

"I killed Gabriel. He didn't organize this. He couldn't."

"No. But he was a cog in a very large organization."

"What does that mean?"

"You know Blackwater and all the other security organizations? This one dwarfs their resources."

"And you sent me to kill their leader?"

"Leader? He was just one of their lieutenants. And we hadn't calculated any blowback as long as everything was done properly. I mean, no one has caught you for any of your other crimes. You're very good at hiding your tracks."

"Are you suggesting they tracked me all the way back to Montréal because of a mistake I made? That's impossible."

"Nothing is impossible. Especially with the resources they have. Did you leave anything at the—uh—the crime scene?"

"The dining scene," I corrected. "I left a good portion of my own blood." I thought a bit longer, reliving the event. Dropping down from the vent. The fight with Gabriel. Saliva when I was talking? No, they wouldn't have any way to track me using my DNA. I wasn't on any donor list. Part way through the confrontation, the guard had come in and I'd kicked him. And broken my shoe. No, not just any shoe. My Edwardian Hamburgers.

I loosened my grip on Dermot.

I remembered reading in the paper that Genevieve, the sales clerk, had been murdered in the shoe store. The place where I'd bought those very shoes. "I left my shoes," I said. Oh, how stupid of me. How very, very stupid. "They tracked the shoes back to a store in Montréal and found my home phone number in their records and used that to figure out my address."

He nodded. "This does seem like an arms dealer's way of sending a message. The bigger the boom, the louder the message. I'm surprised they didn't use a howitzer."

Genevieve had died a horrible death because of my stupidity. An innocent life was lost. She was the closest thing I'd had to a friend. I shook my head, surprised at the emotion welling up in me. I'd sort out my feelings later. I needed answers.

"Why the hell did you come back?" I said. "The contract was done."

"Let's say I didn't agree with the terms handed down from above."

"Was it just a negotiation tactic?" I asked.

"It was a little of both, I guess. You may need our help to survive."

"Well the arms dealers won't be able to track me any further. What's this arms organization called, by the way?"

"ZARC," he said.

"Does that stand for something?" These acronyms were going to drive me crazy.

"No. It's named after the CEO. Anthony Zarc."

I released Dermot. "I'll go underground. I'll be gone."

"In the next few hours, they'll know your body wasn't found. They may know already, depending on how many cops they've bribed."

"I still don't see how they can trace me."

"*We* did. And their resources are much deeper than ours."

He was herding me toward his organization. I also saw that standing inside the store arguing with him, broken glass all around, we were attracting a bit of attention. Sirens were getting closer. I helped him up and we stumbled to the sidewalk.

"Will you trust me once more?" he said.

"No," I answered. "Never."

He pressed a button on the side of his watch. Nothing happened. Then a few seconds later the sirens stopped.

"Was that a coincidence?" I asked.

He shrugged a coy shrug. "You need me, Amber. You need *us*. ZARC will be watching every airport. Every bus station. Every border. We can keep you safe."

"How do I know you won't just stick me in some kind of sick experiment?" I asked.

"You don't," he said. A black car had pulled up beside him,

and the door opened of its own accord. I needed a watch like his: the magic siren-stopping, black-car-summoning watch.

I rocked on my heels. There was a straight line down the sidewalk, then I could duck into an alley and be gone. Forever. But at the last moment, I rubbed the snake ring on my little finger, rocked forward, and stepped inside.

I hoped it wasn't the stupidest choice I'd ever made.

15

The White House

We were whisked out of the city and sped south toward the border. The driver was a Chinese man with a square, bald head who looked like he'd perhaps fought in several of the communist wars, judging by the scars. The driver was now the third person I'd seen from the organization. Well, third if you counted the guy I'd followed in an alley a million years ago.

Dermot was on his smartphone, which looked like it had been designed in the 1980s. He shook it several times, as if expecting that to scramble the words or change whatever text he'd just received.

"What will you offer me?" I asked.

"The same terms as before."

"No, I mean you, Dermot—what will *you* offer me?"

"What do you mean?"

I pointed at him. "You're the only one I know from your organization. I want your word."

"I promise to keep you safe."

"Safe? This girl can look after herself. Promise to find my mother."

"We can't."

"Again, I'm talking only to you. Not your organization. I want you to promise."

He scratched his head. "I'll do my best."

"Promise!"

"I promise to do my best to find your mother," he said. "Is that enough?"

"Good," I said. "At least that's something. I don't even know the name of your organization. I've been calling it the DBI."

"DBI?"

"Yes, Dermot's Bureau of Investigation."

He laughed. "It's a little bigger than that," he said. "We don't have an acronym, though. We just call ourselves the League."

"League of what? Supernerds?"

"Just the League."

"That tells me nothing."

He shrugged. "It's our name, nonetheless. Will you be in league with the League?"

"I want right of refusal on my missions. More control. I don't want them just plopped on my lap. I want choice."

"That can be done. But we need something from you."

"Which is?" I, for some reason, expected him to say genetic material.

"More training. There are some who believe you are a loose cannon. You need to focus."

I bit my tongue. "Yes. I can do that."

"Then it's a deal?"

I looked at him. He was smiling. "Yes," I said after a moment's pause. "For now. You seem to be my best option. By the way, what's the whole point of this organization?"

"To bring peace to mankind," he said. He didn't seem to be

joking.

"What do I care for mankind?"

"You do. I can tell. As much as you try to be cynical."

I snorted.

"Where are we going?" I asked.

"To a safe house in Vermont," Dermot said.

"Ooh, that actually sounds comfortable."

"It'll be adequate to your needs." His stiff and proper English suggested he hadn't spent much time in the real world. Perhaps he was raised from a test tube inside this League of his.

We drove through the Blackpool border crossing into New York state without stopping. Yes, that's right. A lane was made open for us. The border guard at the window didn't even look up, perhaps had been given orders not to look up. Maybe we were invisible.

"That's impressive," I said.

Dermot shrugged. "The perks of being in the League."

I still had to stifle a laugh every time I heard the name of the organization. I imagined a coalition of comic book nerds sitting around arguing about what they wanted to call themselves. "The League! No, the Guild of Do-Gooders."

"I suppose 'Guild of Do-Gooders' was already taken," I said. No sense wasting a clever thought inside my head.

Dermot didn't deign to answer that question.

We went east along several quiet highways, crossing bridges here and there. My eyelids began to droop. Along with my attention span. Blink. Blink. Then came longer periods of darkness. I was rather exhausted—a run up and down a mountain, a near-death experience, a battle with the hairy man next to me ... oh, and I'd had classes that morning. So, I slept.

I awoke with a bit of a start and was momentarily bewildered and short of breath.

"You snore," Dermot said. "Did you know that?"

"I do not!"

"Yes, you do. It wasn't an entirely horrible sound."

"Vampires don't snore," I said. Of course my mother had informed me that I was a Grade A snorer. She had looked into surgery, suggesting that my snores might compromise our ability to hide.

"It's not your least attractive feature," Dermot said.

I laughed.

We wove and weaved and turned our way into Vermont, passing all the stereotypical white houses and pretty little towns. My thoughts returned to Genevieve, and a lead ball of guilt formed in my stomach. My own stupidity had caused her death. I hadn't intended it, of course, but from now on, I needed to be more aware of the ramifications of my actions.

Grief. That's what I was feeling. I'd only known her for half an hour, but she represented so much that I admired in humans. And she'd been snuffed out. Revenge would be a great course of action.

Eventually we drove down a country lane and stopped at an old, white house. It was the perfect place to hide since there were thousands of these houses in Vermont. This one was guarded by a line of white pines and yellow birch and a maple tree in the front yard.

I followed Dermot into the house. "Welcome to the White House," he said as he opened the front door.

"Creative name! I hope your organization is more creative when it comes to hiding its clients."

Inside, the house was warm and homey. The furniture had a

87

bit of a 1950s feel to it: braided rugs on the floor and quilts on the couch. There was a rocking chair next to the fireplace. It appeared to be brand new. He showed me the living room, the washroom, kitchen, then pointed at the door to an office but led me past it.

I smelled other human pheromones and could hear the distant *thud thud* of a heartbeat. "Who's in there?" I asked.

"A friend. Don't worry, you'll be meeting in a few minutes." He led me to an open door. "And here's your room."

It was a large bedroom with a double bed. Several piles of clothing were on it: long sleeved shirts. T-shirts. Blue jeans. Dresses. Even eight boxes of shoes.

"Are those clothes for me?" I asked.

"I took the liberty of calling ahead."

"You know my size?"

"I'm a good guesser."

"Well, that's very thoughtful of you. I'd like some time to freshen up."

"Take all the time you need."

There was an en suite bathroom. A shower rejuvenated me. After drying off, I picked a nice pair of blue jeans and a black sweater that made my pale skin stand out. The clothes fit perfectly. Dermot had a good eye. Or he was a professional dresser in another life.

Dermot was waiting in the living room. He had changed too. I guessed he had his own room there. Or a suitcase in the trunk. "You look better," he said.

"I feel better. Are we roomies?" The possibility was intriguing.

He shook his head. "No. I'm needed at Central. But I do have a surprise."

"I hate surprises."

"Well, it's a good one. The chairman is here to see you."

"Am I that important that I get a visit from one of the bosses?"

"He just happened to be here. The chairman will be out of the office in a moment."

Dermot stood up and headed for the front door.

"Where are you going?" I asked.

"To Central."

"Don't you need to protect your chairman from me?"

"He doesn't need protection." Then Dermot walked out the door.

So much for sappy goodbyes.

I was expecting an old white guy to come out of the office door. Maybe in a wheelchair—one of those comic book clichés. But the door swung open, and the man who came through was black. He was in blue jeans and a dark shirt and looked a little like an African American Steve Jobs.

"So you're Amber Fang," he said. He had a rather deep voice and warm eyes. "It's a pleasure to meet you, Amber." He extended a hand. "I'm Ernest."

I'd been tempted to give a good squeeze but held back. Something about the way he carried himself commanded respect. "Well, it's a pleasure to meet you, Ernest." They certainly had a collection of odd names in this league. "Thank you for pressuring me to rejoin your organization."

"I hope you don't feel it was pressure. I've been very impressed by you."

Most humans are impressed by me nearly came out of my mouth. But I impressed myself by holding it in.

"And what are your intentions with me?" I asked with just

the right amount of demureness.

"Well, we want you to stay here for a short while to continue your studies."

"Studies?"

"Yes, we've arranged an online completion of your courses. We may even be able to give you a practicum in a nearby library. Assuming your marks are high enough." He grinned.

"They will be."

"We have a training regimen for you too," he said. "You've operated on your own for many years. This is a good time to hone your skills. Can you fire a gun?"

"It's not necessary."

"It may become so." He pushed his glasses up, examining me more closely.

"I only kill with my teeth," I said. "I should remind you that I need to eat in about twelve days."

"That will be arranged."

"Is it a delivery service or take out?"

"I'm sorry, but we only do take out," he said. Though he did grin. "Have a good rest, Amber Fang. And welcome to the League."

Then he turned and walked out of the house. As I watched through the window, he got into a black Oldsmobile and drove away. He didn't even have a driver.

He came all this way to see me. That was impressive, yet odd. But perhaps the league's HQ wasn't that far.

I was alone in the house.

So I went to my bed, found a copy of *The Shining* on the bookshelf, and read. Then I fell asleep in my new world.

16

The Big B

Enter boredom.

Well, not complete boredom. I did have several books, a wireless internet connection, and a white personal trainer with the personality of a wet stick, though he was particularly good at martial arts. His head was shaved. His name was Jake, and he didn't live at the White House. He just showed up at the door at ten o'clock every morning, and we went into the walled back yard and fought hand to hand for an hour.

In the afternoons, I continued my Master's in Library Science online from the University of North Texas. Why hadn't I thought of online studies earlier? I should have been taking internet courses my whole life—no human contact to foul things up. In the evenings, I read Stephen King or watched CNN. My first project was a paper on the history of information retrieval systems. I was thinking I'd call it *I Go Boo at Boolean Logic*. Okay, that was only funny to about point one percent of humanity.

A week passed, and I began to get a little nervous about when I'd be eating. That last part of the thirty-day cycle was kind of like smelling meat grilling on a barbecue for a week. I started thinking about blood a lot more and staring at Jake's jugular.

Thankfully, with six days left, I heard the front door open. I ambled out of my room, rubbing the sleep from my eyes. Dermot was there in a gray suit.

"You must be getting hungry," he stated.

"Angry too. Which is part of it. I prefer to know when I'll be eating a bit sooner. I usually have my meals planned out a few weeks in advance."

"We hadn't intended to be working with you again so soon, and it took a bit of organizing to put this one together. The last target was, perhaps, too complicated for you." He paused. Hopefully because of the angry darts shooting out of my eyes. "As a first job, that is."

There was a manila envelope on the rocking chair. I picked it up. "Paper? Envelopes? Why are you so old fashioned?"

"Actually, paper is the hardest to trace. There is only this copy. If you burn it, it no longer exists. Electronic trails exist forever. And information, like a virus, can be transmitted to the wrong people."

"You mean this was typed on a typewriter?" I said.

He nodded.

"By you?"

"By someone in the office. Though I often use a typewriter. And a lot of Wite-Out."

"That is some seriously odd shit you guys do."

I sliced open the envelope with my pinky. I pulled out the papers to discover a photo of an attractive blonde woman in her early thirties. Her bio stated she was an Icelandic librarian.

"Why on earth would I eat her?"

"Keep reading," he said.

Her name was Bjork. Okay, I'm kidding. It was Hallgerdur

Grettirsdottir. How was that for a handle? And she really was a librarian in Reykjavik.

It became clear in the next few paragraphs that she was also the librarian for ZARC, the arms dealer organization that had so recently tried to put me to sleep with a rocket launcher.

"But did she kill someone?" I asked.

He motioned at the paper. "Read on."

"Ah, she's a sniper," I said.

"Yes. She has a preference for a particular type of radium-tipped ammunition. There's a list of our agents who've encountered her." There was a bullet-point list of six agents (three male and three female) and short descriptions of their deaths.

"She's a good shot."

"One of the best in the world."

I picked up the papers. "How can I trust this information?"

"You have to trust us, Amber. These are not the type of people who leave mountains of evidence. She also has information about the holding pen." He said this as if I knew what the holding pen was.

"The holding pen?"

"Yes, the pen in Panama where they interviewed the vampire. She designed it."

"She's an engineer too?"

"She has an impressive variety of skills. She was part of the team that captured the vampire they experimented on. That's what our intelligence suggests, anyway. Her blood is waiting for you. We should have a chance to interview her before ... well ... before your mealtime."

"When do I go?" I asked. I was very hungry. And any scrap of information about my fellow vampires would be helpful. If

93

only my mother hadn't guarded her secrets so closely.

"We leave today," Dermot said.

"We? I work better alone."

"It was decided that you need a—how shall I put it delicately?—a keeper."

"Keeper?"

"Yes. View me as an assistant. You'll like that."

"You can towel my brow when I've finished my job."

Within an hour, we were in a car heading for New York. Then shortly after that, in first class on an Icelandair flight to Reykjavik. I'd never been to Iceland, and I greatly anticipated seeing the land of the sagas. These Icelanders knew how to tell a tale. They did not have any particular vampire mythology, but blood spewed through their stories. And *draugrs* were constantly coming back from the dead. The country had a close to a one hundred percent literacy rate. These were the facts you picked up as a librarian-in-training.

Perhaps their blood was thick with words.

The plane was soon in the heavens. Dermot brought out an e-reader the moment we were at cruising altitude. It was odd to see him with an electronic device. "What are you reading?" I asked.

"Descartes," he said.

"Oh, now you're just trying to impress me."

"No. I find it relaxing."

"I just want to break things when I read Descartes. Like his head. But anyway, to each her own."

He nodded. He turned out to be a rather boring travel mate. I read the on-flight magazine, did a few hours of homework, and watched a movie before we landed.

17

The Dance Floor

Keflavik International Airport had a red roof. Oh, and lots of glass. It was also shrouded in that fog and mist that had come out of the pages of the sagas and had been hanging around since the longships first brought the Vikings' beating hearts to this countryside.

We landed safely and went through security without a problem. I'd expected to see blonde women and men everywhere—another stereotype, I knew—but most of the women had dark hair. The men were tall. And plenty of camera-clad tourists were scrambling for their buses. Iceland was a photographer's mecca. It was like a gorgeous green spot on the moon.

"Why don't we go there first?" I pointed at a sign for a place called Blue Lagoon, a hot spring. The people in the image looked happy and well-heated. The water was an unbelievable shade of light blue.

"There's no time," Dermot said. "We have much to do before our work is done."

"Is that some sort of Zen koan?"

"No. I just want you to concentrate on why we're here."

"Okay, Mr. Fuddy Duddy, lead on."

We took a cab down the highway to Reykjavik, passing the American military base on our way. Soon, we were in the city itself. It wasn't the largest city in the world, but it made up for that by being colorful. The houses were red, pale green, white, and yellow—bright colors that shimmered in the sun. I liked that the Icelanders weren't afraid to be bold with their paint. We passed near Hallgrímskirkjachurch with its giant tower that reminded me of pipe organs. It dominated the skyline of the city.

The cab stopped at Hotel Borg, an art deco hotel that stood out because of its gray and white walls. We checked in, then went into the silver-doored elevator and up to the fifth floor.

"Have a rest," Dermot said. It was 8:00 p.m. Icelandic time.

"Is that an order? I hear the Icelanders party like it's 1299."

"Rest. Any irregularities could draw attention to us."

"It's not like I'm going to get drunk and start a brawl."

He raised an eyebrow. It reminded me of a look my mom would give—that exasperated *How did I get stuck with her?* look. It was a little bit odd and frightening, and endearing.

And totally aggravating.

"We've spent six hours on a plane, and I want to stretch my legs. Join me, Dermot. Cast off your fuddy duddy ways."

"I have paperwork."

"Paperwork? You didn't even bring your typewriter."

He grimaced. "Just be careful. This isn't a holiday."

"Okay, Mom."

I went into my room. We were on the top floor, so the roof curved over a large bed with a white comforter and a black headboard. There was a picture of a man and a goat on the wall.

I freshened up, and one elevator ride later, I was marching

along the street. There had been a rain—or more correctly, a thick, drenching mist—but it had cleared after painting the streets with moisture.

The truth was, I needed to walk because the blood lust, *the curse* as Mom used to call it, was boiling in my blood. Walking distracted me.

I passed several restaurants. I missed a lot of the culture of any country because food was so intertwined with the human experience. In Iceland, they had an island mentality to food: they were willing to eat anything. Shark. Puffin. Cheeses. But it was all lost on me. Even the smells didn't mean much. A hot dog, or lobster with butter, or a soufflé—all the same. They weren't blood.

Suffice to say, I never watched cooking shows.

Anyway, culture was also art and dance and music, and I hadn't been to a bar since my time in Seattle, so I went through a wooden door into Café Amsterdam. There was a band throat-roaring black metal in German, or maybe it was Norwegian. People were dancing madly. I walked right in, threw my coat on a chair, and joined the throng. Dancing was something I was damn good at.

Twenty minutes passed. The bass made my heart beat faster, made my body feel more primal. If there was one thing I could thank humans for, it was creating music. And amplifiers. I forgot who I was. What I was doing there. And I danced. The throng thronged. Most of the people were in their twenties and all vibrantly dancing on this island on the edge of forever.

A man with an ankh earring briefly danced with me. But I turned away, and when I turned back again, he was gone. I was glad for that because I'd started to stare at his neck.

You know, on that point, we didn't always go for the neck.

It was just the easiest to reach. There was the femoral vein in the thigh that was handy. And the brachial veins in either arm. These exterior veins were very difficult to bite into, though, and it was harder to hold your food down while you were eating and waiting for the sleep agent to reach their brain. All that kicking and thrashing could lead to an upset stomach.

The ankh-eared man came back, this time a little more red-eyed, and got near enough that he was leaning over me. I felt his slobbering lips on my neck. I reached down and quickly pinched one of his testicles, and he was on the floor in agony. I danced my way into the crowd. I didn't see him again. I just danced. Eventually, the band grunted twice loudly and took a break.

As I grabbed my coat, a table of three women nearby gave me the thumbs up. A sign of solidarity. Obviously, they'd had encounters with ankh man.

One said something to me in Icelandic, and I shrugged and said, "I don't speak your language."

"Oh, you speak English," a blonde said.

"Yes. My native tongue."

"Well, join us for a drink, and we'll toast your native tongue."

This was not what I'd promised Dermot. This was not lying low.

"He was my ex-boyfriend," another said. "The man you put on the floor."

"Sorry to hear that."

This got a laugh. "Where are you from?" the blonde asked.

"Kansas," I said.

They motioned for me to sit. I did so and took the proffered glass of wine. The women had fine jugulars and angular, classically beautiful faces. They asked me questions about my life in Kansas, so I made up answers. We were joined by an attractive, blond, straight-jawed man who didn't seem to have any romantic connections to the women. His eyes were a lively blue, and his sweater an unlively gray. His name was Halldór. All four of them were students at Reykjavík University.

"What I'd like to know about is GKS 2365 4to," I said. I smiled a bit. I was testing them. And this was a test only a librarian would think of. The women gave me blank stares. But Halldór grinned.

"The Codex Regius of the Poetic Edda?" he said. "At the Árni Magnússon Institute?" The three women tapped their foreheads. "You have a passion for old books?"

It was one of the oldest books in the world—ancient Norse poems about gods and such. "Yes, I'd like to dance around those ancient words."

"No dancing there," Halldór said.

"There isn't a place in the world where I can't dance," I said. "We can dance on the rooftop. I'll show you."

He stood and the other three laughed as if a bet had been won. We left the club and walked toward the Institute.

And, purely by chance, we walked by *Landsbókasafn Íslands - Háskólabókasafn*, the National and University Library of Iceland. It was a rectangular, red building, with a white elevator shape on either side. They did like their primary colors here.

Tomorrow, I would dine there.

"You like the library?" he asked.

"Yes. Books feed my soul." The wine was obviously getting to me. "Well, maybe I can't dance in there."

"You said you can dance anywhere."

"I'm a better private dancer."

This got him to raise an Icelandic eyebrow. "That can be the best type."

"Then I'll go see the Poetic Edda tomorrow." Again, you weren't supposed to play with food, but it was nice to talk. Turns out he was writing a play, but he also ran a tourist company specializing in saga-related tours.

"Back up a bit," I said. "The sagas are stories. How can you visit them?"

"Well, you can go to the places where the events were supposed to have taken place. Whether they actually happened or not, that is in the mist of history."

I must admit, I liked that phrase. It warmed the cockles of my librarian heart.

So I said, "Come back to my room with me."

He kept a calm face and his heartbeat sped up only slightly. We vampires could be rather forward.

"It would be my pleasure."

Hand in hand—mine cold, his warm—we went back to the Hotel Borg, through the silver doors, and up in the elevator. Just as we came to my door, the one across the hall opened and Dermot stepped out.

"Amber," he said. "What are you doing?"

"I went out," I said. "I came back. I made a friend. Sorry, Mom."

There was a look on his face that I couldn't quite place. Consternation. Something possessive, maybe. Then he glanced at Halldór, who had extended his hand to shake. Dermot didn't take it. "We'll continue this discussion in the morning," he said.

"Yes, Mom," I said.

Then I pulled Halldór into my room and closed the door.

"Who was that?" Halldór asked.

"Oh, my colleague. Another librarian."

"He was not happy."

"He rarely is," I said. Then I cranked on the old radio and tuned it to a station that was playing some odd, ghostly-sounding folk music. I kissed Halldór and tried to ignore the blood rushing in his veins.

Halldór paused long enough to say, "Your colleague isn't going to be mad, is he?"

"Forget about him," I said. "Forget about everything. That's what I'm going to do."

And we did forget about everything.

18

Compromising the Compromised

"You compromised the mission," Dermot said. These accusing words were shot at me over a plate of eggs and something the Icelanders called *skyr*, a white, yogurt substance. Dermot was eating it. I was drinking Icelandic coffee. It was very tasty and making my heart go *ba dump dump dump*. Not blood tasty, of course. But I did need to stay hydrated.

"I entertained myself."

"Spending that much time with a local. What do you think will happen when they find our target dead? He'll have your face in his memory. This isn't a big community. They're all related to each other."

"What's Halldór going to tell them? Besides, no one took a photograph of me."

"That you know of," he said. He set down his utensils. "You don't understand how serious this is, do you? You nearly died because you left a shoe at your last elimination scene. A woman in Montréal was murdered because of that mistake. Horribly. And now you spend time with a local. What if our mission is not successful? And ZARC tracks him down? How do think they'll treat him?"

Now that he was listing my transgressions, I was feeling a little stupid. But I bit my lip.

"No one will identify me," I said.

"Did you tell him where you were from?"

"Kansas," I said. "It's a Wizard of Oz reference."

"Clever. So they know you're North American."

"There are thousands of North Americans here. We've flooded this country with our cameras."

"Yes, but you're rather memorable. And certainly to him. He got to know you *intimately*." He nearly spat out that last word.

"Well, I probably shouldn't mention that we walked by the library last night."

"You did what?"

"It was by accident." It dawned on me that maybe I shouldn't have been making any decisions right after dancing my heart out and drinking wine.

"So when the body turns up and the papers go haywire, he won't remember that the strange woman from Kansas showed interest in the library. There are very few murders here. They make a splash."

"He wouldn't put two and two together. His hormones were shutting down his brain."

"He knows what hotel you're in. Even what room. And he's seen me."

"I told him you were another librarian and we were here for a conference."

"And when he discovers there is no conference?"

"You worry too much, Dermot." I drained the coffee cup. I was feeling several shades of stupid. I'd become lax. It was as if in ceding control to the League, I'd let down my guard.

A few moments of simmering silence passed. Dermot was

staring at me the whole time.

"Are you trying to burn a hole in my forehead?" I asked.

"Well, the mission is done."

"What?"

"It's been compromised in far too many ways. We can't continue."

"You aren't serious."

"No," he said. "I am serious. We are in the fallback position thanks to you. I stuck my neck out to get you back into the League, and this is how you repay me."

"It wasn't intentional. And we can't go. I need to feed."

"We'll find a secondary target in the United States."

"I could just feed on you."

He narrowed his eyes. "Your threats aren't entertaining. And your lack of remorse and inability to admit responsibility is noted."

Noted. That stung. "Listen, we can find this Hallgerdur Grimdaughter, and we can eliminate her."

"Not in the library."

"Then somewhere else," I said.

"There is no time to work up another plan."

"We can adapt."

"And compromise this mission even further?"

"No." I reached across and took his hand. Gently. "Dermie." Okay that wasn't a good way to start. "Dermot, I mean. I—I know I was stupid. I didn't think things out properly. It's the blood, the need to eat." I was looking at his neck. I turned my gaze to his eyes. His angry, cold eyes. "I made several mistakes. Stupid ones, I freely admit that. In fact, I won't go out or do anything from here on without your permission. But we can complete this. I can get into any building. That part is easy for me."

The steely look in his eyes hadn't softened. What did a girl have to do? Cry? Ha, that would be the day.

"Do you know where she lives?" I asked.

He nodded. Gee, he didn't even want to speak. Maybe inside his Old Mother Hubbard brain, he was seeing some of my logic.

"I want to make this up to you. We can check out her lodging. Remember, I can get into a prison undetected."

"I need to get in too. We need to question her."

"Well, we'll work on that. I'll unlock the front door. Assuming she doesn't live in a cave."

"We'll stay one more night," he said. "We'll visit her home, and we'll see. That's all ... we'll see."

"You're a good sport, Dermot," I said. I gave him my friendliest smile.

He didn't smile back.

19

The Hit Begins

It turned out, Hallgerdur lived on top of Mount Doom.

It was a short trip out of Reykjavik on a typical, lonely stretch of mist-covered highway. Her house had been built atop a cliff. It was a plethora of windows and stone and heated by steam like most everything in that country. For someone living on a librarian's salary, she had deep pockets. She must have charged a truckload of coin per kill.

"Wow," I said. "Now that's a house."

"Yes, and she designed it herself," Dermot said. "She's very talented."

"It's almost as if you have a thing for her."

He shrugged. "That's been over for ten years. Work relationships are bad for work."

"What? You mean she worked for the League and you two ..." I couldn't find the right word. It was hard to imagine. "Dated?"

"That isn't pertinent information."

"You mean you came along on this mission and she could recognize you? You're jeopardizing the mission by your very presence." I was especially proud of that last line.

"I have a different face."

We pulled up to the base of the rocky hill and parked.

"A different face? What does that mean?"

"Exactly that. I had different features. There was a ... an accident. And I went through some alterations."

"Did you look better or worse?" I asked.

"Better," he said.

"I'm wondering if I'd like your other face more. Do you happen to have a picture?"

"No."

"Well, someday, I'd really like to see a snapshot. Were you two lovers?"

"We had common goals," he said.

"Wow, how romantic. And what happened? She broke your typewriter?"

"She changed," he said. "That's what happened."

It sounded like every relationship I'd seen in a soap opera. Not that I had anything to judge in real life, having really only had a relationship with my mother and an aborted date in high school that ended with me almost tearing the boy's head off (and a quick move to another state).

"In what way," I asked, "did she change?"

"This isn't pertinent to the operation," he replied gruffly. And maybe with *un soupçon* of petulance. "She used to be you."

Ah, now I was getting the picture. Long ago, the League had a sniper who could kill from a distance. A very effective sniper. And now she was playing for the other team.

"So I'm her replacement. Oh, this is juicy. I'm about to go and ... what? Give her a pink slip?"

"No. We've had several, uh, eliminators since that time." I made a note to find out what had happened to them. "She's just another target."

"Listen, if I'm going to be draining your ex-girlfriend, that's pertinent information. I need to know how you'll react. She's rather attractive, so I'm confused about one thing."

"What?"

"Why would she be interested in you?"

He barked out a laugh. "You do like to lash out. But I looked different then, remember. I was, perhaps, a different man. Maybe more headstrong. But things changed after the … the accident." He glanced at his watch. "We need to get into her house."

"You keep referring to an accident. But I think it may not have been an accident."

"That also isn't pertinent information. Let's concentrate on our task instead of playing twenty questions."

"By my count, I'm only up to seven questions. I have thirteen more. I'll ask them later." The only road up was certainly being watched by cameras. I glanced at the slick rock walls. "I'll have to climb," I said.

He eyed the rock through the window. It was wet with Atlantic drizzle. Iceland seemed to have the market on drizzle and fog. And chill. "You can climb that?"

"It will be a breeze," I said. "The hard part will be doing it without sweating."

I stepped out of the vehicle and tightened my blue rain slicker. He rolled down his window. "Be safe, Amber," he said.

"That's a silly thing to say, but thanks, Mom," I answered. His concern was making me a little nervous.

I was, after all, about to climb seventy-five feet up a mist-covered, cliff wall with cold hands. And my fingers were trembling. Was I just doing this to show off for him?

The ascent was not as easy as I'd hoped. I'd climbed plenty

of buildings, and my nails were rather good for digging in, and I was wearing good shoes with nice, bendable toes. But it was slick and cold and, so forbidding that I slipped. The first time, I was about ten feet up and lost my grip with one hand and had to grab and stab the other hand into the rock, chipping away a few stones.

I had two more near-death experiences at about the fifty-five-foot mark. My hands were getting colder. And, frankly, I was starving. Everything became a tad more difficult when you were hungry. The timing of this mission was a little too late in my feeding cycle. I should've had a meal a day or two before to think rationally. Instead, all I could picture was her neck. Her pale, luscious neck. The prospect of eating gave me a bit more strength, and I climbed the next twenty feet quickly and without incident.

Ten minutes later, I was at the top. I paused to wave to Dermot. The adrenaline made my wave look like a palsy. Then I glanced across the horizon, the light of Reykjavik in the distance. And I pictured myself at a desk in Montréal or Seattle or Boston, looking for my next meal. Was I really the same person who wasted so much time flipping through court documents?

I peeked my head over a stone parapet and got a clearer view of the house. A few lights were on. The whole side of the rectangular house was glass and misted, so I couldn't see in clearly, though I did glimpse Hallgerdur moving from one room to another.

There were plenty of heads staring in my direction.

Animal heads. On the wall of her living room. There was a veritable menagerie of beasts of prey: lions, tigers—name a predator and it was there, staring with glassy eyes. Even a crocodile. So Miss Sniper didn't just hunt humans. And she liked to keep her trophies on the wall. I wouldn't have been surprised to see a human head or two. Maybe she kept those in the basement.

I scanned for cameras or motion detectors. The little infrared lights were very easy to spot. And to avoid. I marked three of them.

A dog was out patrolling, but as I had no scent and made no noise, it was as if I didn't exist for the dog.

I chose a part of the house that wasn't all glass. I skittered across the rock garden and climbed up to the second story, which was another layer of glass. She certainly didn't mind people looking in. Then again, she was on the tallest part of the rock and the nearest house was a mile down the road. Someone would have to be in a helicopter to spy on her. I thought about the psychology of a sniper who liked to look in every direction as far as the eye could see.

I crawled onto the balcony, stepping down on a marble chair. I supposed this is where she drank her coffee and watched the sun rise. Or read her books—being a librarian and all that. I wondered if we'd get time to talk about our favorite reads. Maybe I'd get a recommendation or two before I ate her.

There was likely an alarm on the sliding door. And motion detectors. These things always made it a little bit difficult to break in. And I assumed someone who worked for a security firm would have the latest in security hardware and software. So far, so good though.

I used a fingernail to etch out a large square in the window. There was the occasional blackboard-type squeak, which set my nerves on edge. I'd never liked that sound. Especially when it might have alerted my target.

The trick was to catch the glass before it fell to the floor and shattered. I'd done this before, but not with such thick glass. I guessed it was bulletproof.

I cut through the last layer, and as the glass fell into the room, I snatched at it. My reflexes, as I've said, were amazing, but I wasn't able to catch it until it was a quarter of an inch from the marble floor. I wiped the sweat from my forehead.

I crawled into the darkened room expecting alarms to go off. It was her bedroom, judging by the white cover on the bed. I crept across a stone floor—a polar bear rug keeping my tread quiet and my feet warm. What hadn't she killed? I liked to hunt. There was a wonderful rush of euphoria in the moment of capture. But I didn't respect those who killed to show their dominance. It was pointless and cried out for psychotherapy. Kill to eat. That was my motto. I could be showing my dominance every day of my life. But there was no joy in that.

Dermot obviously had poor taste. Or he was different before the so called "accident."

Anyway, I was tempted to just kill her and feed, but he needed to question her. Why did he have to make everything so complicated? Although, if she did have answers to a few of his questions about the universe—specifically about my kind—well, I wanted to know those answers too.

I cocked an ear. She'd been downstairs, but in the time it had taken to cut through the window, she could've gone anywhere. A TV was on somewhere on the lower floor. Maybe she was watching Icelandic soaps. I'd flip off the alarm, then call Dermot up. Of course, I'd have to subdue her first, but that would be the easy part. I mean, she may have been a sniper, but she shouldn't be anywhere near as fast or strong as I was. The

augmented, either by Gabriel's organization or another one.
When the questioning was done, maybe I'd feed on her right in
front of all the stuffed predator heads. I smiled and licked my
lips.

I slowly, so slowly opened the door to the main room.

And looked face-to-barrel with a .45 Magnum.

20

The Hit Continues

Her hand was perfectly still. Her eyes were blue, just as the picture promised. And she was watching me with a curious diffidence.

"Give me three good reasons why I shouldn't blow your head off." Her voice was calm and elegant and contained a hint of an accent.

Three reasons? I swallowed. "One: if you shoot me, you won't know why I'm here. Two: you'd get your polar bear rug all stained with brains and blood. That can't be easy to clean. And three ..." I had just impressed myself—I'd rattled those first two off without hesitation. I needed a kicker for the ending. "Oh, Dermot says hello."

Watching her reaction was interesting. She nodded at the first point, nearly smiled with the second point, then with the last point, her eyes opened slightly wider. I had her. She wasn't going to pull that trigger. At least not right away.

Now, I could have attempted to disarm her. But there was always a slight chance that contact would press her finger against the trigger. My thoughts would be splattered against a rather nicely painted wall.

Never let them shoot your brains out, Mom had told me every morning. Okay, she'd never said that one. But it was a motto for me, ever since my heinous hit on that mafia kingpin in Boston.

"Dermie," she whispered.

"Is that your pet name for him?"

Hallgerdur's eyes froze into Icelandic ice. "So the League has finally come to erase their rogue agent. Nice try. What are they paying you?"

"I'm pretty cheap, I must admit. A meal. A glass of wine. A holiday in a sunny place."

I thought I was being flip and clever, but her eyebrows rose an eighth of an inch and she said, "So *you* killed Gabriel. Our little vampire hit girl. I should have known." She set the barrel of the gun right against my forehead. "Don't think you can react fast enough to stop me from pulling the trigger."

Stupid. Stupid me. This Hallgerdur was a little bit too clever for her own good. Well, for *my* own good. Maybe Dermot was right: I needed more training. I just wasn't used to talking to my food.

"Come this way." She grabbed my shoulder and guided me over to a white chair. My dirty rain slicker would stain it with mud and water. She used the barrel of the gun to push me into a seated position. Then she backed slowly away and sat across the room. The gun was perfectly level the whole time. "How long have you worked for the League?"

"Oh, a bit here and a bit there," I said.

"You've convinced yourself that you're clever. You've spent too much time alone. Most of your kind are like that."

"My kind? How many do you know?"

"I have known three," she said. The *have known* was a little bit ominous. Frustrating to think that she had already known more vampires than me. "You're the youngest I've seen. I thought your species was dying out. I guess someone managed to reproduce."

All new information to me. "I spring from fertile loins."

"The League's methods of capture must have improved. Were you supposed to ask me any questions? Or were you just going to drain my blood and leave me here?"

"I was supposed to challenge you to game of checkers."

She shot me. The bullet went right through the flesh of my shoulder and into the chair. "Damn it!" I said. I squeezed my shoulder with my left hand. Blood stained my hands. There was a hole through my rain slicker, the blood coming down the blue fabric and spreading across her white chair. "Awww. Ouch!" I bit my lip. "I'm staining your chair."

"I'll buy a new one," she said. "I'm not in the mood for jokes. That was a clear shot. I didn't aim for any bone. Your kind heal quickly. What were your orders?"

"A short conversation then lunch," I hissed between clenched teeth.

"Please be forthright and more explicit with your answers."

Wow, she sounded so official. Blood kept trickling out, and damn did the wound ever hurt.

"How many kills have you performed for the League?"

"One," I said.

"Gabriel was your first?"

"Yes. And don't you think the League is a rather silly name? I mean, it's not very creative is it?"

I think I was maybe getting a little delirious. By her hard stare, I assumed she was deciding whether or not to shoot me again.

"Uh, please continue with the questions," I said. The blood

leaking out of my body and my yearning to consume someone else's blood were hammering at any sane thoughts. *Pull yourself together, Amber,* I thought. I could make a leap for her, but she could fire before that, and this time not to wound. If I dodged to the side, maybe the bullet would miss. But now that I was wounded, my reaction time would be slower.

"What's your name?" she asked.

"Alicia Von Stratton." Where that came from, I don't know. Now I'd just have to remember that name. Alice?

"And what strain of vampire are you?" she asked.

"Strain? There are different strains?"

She nodded as if I'd answered a question.

"How did Dermot survive?" she asked.

I blinked. "Survive what?"

She nodded. Had I given something away? Only that I didn't know very much. Which meant I might get shot at any moment. My guess was there'd be no warning before the shot. Just *bang.* So I wouldn't be able to react. Again, I noted how steady the barrel was. She must have worked out. "Why didn't he change his name? He's always such a stickler. So stodgy."

"Oh, I agree," I said. I was willing to agree with most everything. "He's totally stodgy. I bet he flosses after every meal."

"Are you as stupid as you're acting?" she asked.

I set my teeth.

"No," she answered her own question. "They just haven't trained you well enough. You're rough around the edges. I see that what happened in Dubai was beginner's luck. A sign of how desperate the League is. When you don't come back, they'll have no eliminators. That's my guess. Apparently, if you cut off the head, the body will die."

Had someone's head been cut off? An electronic warning bell rang. She looked to her left—a screen flared to life on the wall, but I couldn't see what it was showing from this angle. "So you're not alone," she said. "Someone got the dogs. Hmmm. I do hope it really is Dermot. Well, you're—"

I knew the period at the end of that sentence was going to be a bullet, so I launched myself to the left. Hot lead whizzed right past my shoulder and through the chair. She spun the gun toward me with such speed it was clear she'd been augmented. Her next shot grazed my leg.

The glass window broke behind her, and Dermot—stodgy, wonderful Dermot—came bounding through. Exactly where he'd jumped from, I couldn't say. He had his own gun drawn. His landing was a little ungainly, but he knocked Hallgerdur to the floor. Her gun rolled one way. His the other. And they rolled together.

Neither gun had ended up near me, which was maybe for the best. I would have ended up shooting them both. That would have solved a lot of my problems.

She raked his face with her nails, four streaks of blood appearing from his eyebrows down his cheeks. I decided to make it a *ménage à trois*. I stood up to do so, but the blood loss had made me dizzy, and I zigged where I should have zagged and ended up on the floor again. I took a deep breath and slowly rose to my feet. Stupid blood. Stupid light-headedness. I really wanted to take her head off.

She made a neat little move and flipped Dermot, sending him through a glass table. She attempted a kung fu chest stomp, but I intercepted her. I'd intended to wrap my arms around her but misjudged. Instead, she was sent sprawling into a bookcase.

"Take that you b—" I began.

She was reaching into a drawer. Oh, why had I paused to say something dramatic? I threw myself at her as she turned a smaller gun toward me and got off a shot that hit me somewhere in the midsection. The wound didn't stop me. I was on her, knocking the gun from her hand and falling across her, her blows hitting my head. I bit into her leg, and she screamed. I was going for the femoral artery, but she smacked me hard enough that my head rang like the Liberty Bell, and was likely just as cracked. Even with my wounds, I was stronger than her. She kept whipping her head from side to side, thrashing. I saw an opening and sank my teeth into her neck. I felt that warm sluice of blood and drank heavily as the paralytic agent from my teeth slipped into her. She stopped thrashing, took a deep breath, and was still. The meal was mine.

The first gulp was always the best. Every cell on my tongue, in my throat, throughout my body was screaming out for this meal. She was a delicious, salty wine. It tasted as though the blood was going straight to my brain. The second gulp was warm and beautiful. The third was—

"No! Stop!" the words were somewhere in a dream kingdom far, far away from my meal, from her life going into mine. I ignored the voice. It was so distant.

Then fireworks exploded in my skull.

21

A Second Helping

I had only been interrupted while feeding once before. A frumpy woman had found me on her husband's neck and she, well, she thought we were making love. An understandable conclusion since he was naked. I was fully clothed, but some people liked doing it that way. She had yanked me off, shouting, "Get away from my husband, you tramp!"

And that's when the blood rage took over. I tossed her through a window, and she landed on the lawn of their suburban home. Then I finished the meal. I should explain her husband was a bad cop. To be honest, I never knew whether she survived that flight. By the time I was done feeding, there were sirens, and I fled the scene with a man-sized portion of blood in my stomach.

"What the hell are you doing?" I snarled.

The rage was right on the edge of my fingernails. I was already closing in on Dermot. He was holding a stool and looking rather sheepish.

"We need her alive," he said.

"She's my meal," I spat. Well, actually it came out more like: *"Shesmymealdiediedie!"* I slashed out at him. *"Diediedie!"*

He held the stool up and blocked my blow, but the stool broke in half. I was seeing red, and if not for my own blood loss, I would've likely started a full-fledged fight. But I slipped in my own blood, most of which was coming out of the hole in my side. More fireworks went off in my skull.

He was above me now. Same sheepish look on his face.

"We need to take her back alive. The mission has changed."

I crouched to leap at him, but my vision was blurred. There were two stupid Dermots looking down at me. Which one had interrupted my meal? I rubbed the side of my head.

"You can change the mission just like that?"

"That's my prerogative."

"I need to finish feeding. I need her blood. Now. That's my prerogative."

"Take mine," he said.

Had seeing her face made him go crazy?

"You'll die."

"No. You can control yourself."

"But if I don't finish the feed, I don't reset my clock."

"We'll figure that out. I'll put a team on it."

I was leaking blood, and an interrupted meal had only made me hungrier. It was illogical. But I needed to finish eating. Now.

"I can't."

"You can, Amber. I know it." He set down the remains of the stool. "At least, I'm pretty sure."

"You're showing a lot of faith in a vampire."

"You're one vampire I trust. You have to promise me you won't use the paralytic agent."

"I can't control its release."

"You don't know that. You've never tried." Then he bent his

neck to one side. "It's important that we preserve her."

"Do you still love her?" I asked.

"No. Never." He gave a fake laugh. "She has more informa-tion that we need. My relationship with her is long over."

The lady—or in this case the man—doth protest too much, I thought.

He wasn't making much sense, but I decided I couldn't wait. And I sank my teeth into his neck and tried to think thoughts like *no paralytic agent no no,* and he grimaced a bit. You know how mosquitos released an anticoagulant? Well, mine didn't seem to be working. His blood didn't flow all that well, and I had to, well, I had to suck quite a bit more than I was used to. It sounded like a symphony of soup slurps. He was wearing cologne and smelled of sweat. But all humans smelled of sweat. I did like the smell. The coppery taste of blood was rich in my mouth.

I closed my eyes and fed. When I opened them again, a year could have passed. But I felt stronger. I looked down at Dermot. He was pale and dead-looking. Either I couldn't control the paralytic agent, or I'd fed too long. I was a little drunk from all that blood. And I'd gained a few pounds.

I slowly, so slowly put my hand on his neck. Feeling for a pulse. Nothing. I'd taken too much.

"Damn," I whispered. "Damn. Damn."

Then the slightest of movements under my index finger. A pulse.

I sat back and sucked in a breath. I'd stopped bleeding. And since the bullet had gone right through my shoulder, I'd be left with a nice circular scar. The bullet in my midsection had also gone through flesh.

Hallgerdur certainly knew how to make an impression.

Oh, and she was gone. I'd thought the paralytic agent would leave her unconscious for hours, but I'd only ever drank until they were dead.

I lurched along the hallway, following the Rorschach-like blood splashes. Across the room. Down the stairs. I paused and peered down the stairwell, listening. Not a noise. How long had I been in my feeding daze? And why, oh, why had evolution given me that little post-feeding period of dullness? Or it was the loss of my own blood causing such slow reactions? I was surprised I could walk at all.

I crept down to the bottom of the stairs, clinging to the wall, and peeked around the corner. Behold—a kitchen with more stainless steel than a starship: fridge, oven, sink, microwave. There was a pear and a half-eaten fish on a plate on a marble table. We'd interrupted her dinner, so I guess it was only fair my own dinner was interrupted.

Anyway, the droplets led to the center of the room. I was still a little blurry, and it hurt to walk, but I followed the trail. There were several paintings on the walls, but I didn't have time to admire them. And all along the opposite wall were rows and rows of books in a rather impressive system of floating shelves.

The blood droplets stopped at the bookcase. She had stood in place, for there was quite the crimson puddle. But she had vanished. It was as if someone had come along, wrapped her wound up, and carried her away. I blinked. Either she had staunched the blood flow and kept walking, or she really had vanished.

It took a second for me to put it together. I couldn't smell her. Or any other human pheromones. There was the slightest red palm print on a book called *Grettis saga Ásumdarsonar,* so she had leaned there. Seeing that classic got my librarian's envy fired up. She owned the book in hardcover! She was reading the Icelandic sagas in German. This woman had quite the brain.

I paused again, and a tiny bulb in my brain glowed with dull light. I pushed on the book. It went into the wall, and the bookshelf opened silently, revealing a doorway and a set of carved-stone stairs leading into what I could only call a cavern. Blood dotted the stone steps.

I started a very careful and slow descent.

22

The Cavern of Surprises

There was a rasping noise from somewhere below—her last breaths? *Careful is as careful does.* That was another Mom-ism. I'd just stopped bleeding. No sense in getting shot again.

So I crept down stair by stair, the steps perfectly smooth. The basement had been dug directly into the rock. Now that was impressive.

It dawned on me that my legs would be first to be seen and the first part of me to be shot. I didn't want any damage to my limbs. So I jumped to the ceiling and dug my claws in. If I'd been at my physical peak, this would have been the simplest of maneuvers. But I banged my head, then nearly slipped. Chunks of rock fell down the steps, alerting whoever was down there to my presence. I took a deep breath and slowly, so slowly turned myself around and crawled spider-like down the ceiling.

My whole plan was to not give her much of a target to shoot at. All I needed to do was peek around the room. It seemed to make sense, but I had about ten pounds of extra blood in me, and that was making it hard to hold on to the solid rock. My sore shoulder didn't help. I creepy-crawled upside down and peeked over the edge of the ceiling.

This would give her only part of my forehead and eyeball to aim at.

Everything was upside down. This room was so deep in the rock that some part of me expected to see the Batmobile and a Batman outfit in a glass case in the middle of the room. There was what looked to be a large rectangular holding cell in one corner. A medical desk and a stainless steel filing cabinet in the other. And several scientific type machines—even a few test tubes.

No sign of Hallgerdur. I peeked again.

A bullet chipped off a chunk of stone and knocked into my cheek, blood spraying to the floor. I tried to lurch backward but lost my hold and fell to the stone stairs, bashing my head. I lurched and rolled to one side—avoiding another shot—and lurched the other way. My eyes blurred. I saw the flash of a muzzle. Hallgerdur was crouched behind a filing cabinet, one hand holding bandages to her neck. I went one way, then another, and she got off two more shots. I had a glimpse of just the flashes and her face, which looked pained and beautiful.

Couldn't this woman just do me the courtesy of dying?

I slammed into a chair and table next. I decided, perhaps stupidly, to be aggressive and flipped up and rammed into the filing cabinet in front of her, knocking it over. Then I ran around the other side.

Hallgerdur was flattened beneath the cabinet, the gun still in her hand. She seemed to be out cold. I kicked the gun away. She was pale as white paper. Her neck was clearly visible, and her heartbeat pulsed there. I wanted to finish the job. To put an end to her and any chance that she would come back. It wasn't like Dermot could stop me. I wasn't sure how she'd dragged herself down here with so little blood in her system.

"You're a tough Viking to kill," I said.

I bent toward her neck. I licked my lips and felt my incisors extend. Ah, but ol' Dermie would get that sad puppy-dog look in his face.

"You don't know how lucky you are." I tied her up using shipping tape from the desk. A lot of it. And wrapped it around her shoulders and legs too, enough that FedEx could have taken her as a parcel. Then I left her there.

What the hell *was* this place? There was a flat-screen monitor on the desk, along with several papers. And, of course, the metal cubicle at one side of the room. Was this a place to interrogate prisoners without the outside world hearing their screams?

I peeked into the bulletproof glass of the holding cell. The bed had been slept in recently, or at least, it hadn't been made since the last occupant. There was an open book on the table, a cup of java beside it. Curious, whoever had been in here had left their book unread, walked out, and slammed the door.

Then a face rose up from behind the glass. I pulled back. A pale man with dark, close-cropped hair and gray eyes. He was in his mid-forties, angular and slim. His grin was devilish.

"Now that was an impressive display," he said. His voice was muffled by the thickness of the glass. A card on the door: *Subject X11123*.

"Thanks," I said. "Who the hell are you?"

"You can call me Martin. That's my first name. I must say I enjoyed your little battle, but you let her live."

"She does have a habit of not staying dead," I said.

"Believe me, I know that."

"And why are you locked in this cage, Marty?"

"I am of great interest and value to the company. I think

that's how she put it. And I'm a stupid, greedy little boy. I got caught eating."

He smiled, showing fangs as sharp and perfect as mine.

23

I Ask Again: Who the Hell?

He leered at me for a long time. I was standing before another vampire. I'd never seen any neck biter other than my mother, and some part of my brain was beginning to believe they didn't exist. I mean, I knew *I* existed, but if you didn't see another vampire, could you really believe? He'd let his incisors retreat back into his mouth.

"Who the hell are you?" I asked.

"You're repeating yourself. I'm Martin. I mentioned that only a few short moments ago. Perhaps you have early onset Alzheimer's."

He emanated confidence. And a very large ego.

"I would like to know how you got here, Martin."

"Well, open the door, and we can have a friendly chat. *Tête à tête*, so to speak. Vampire to vampire."

"I'm a little tired, Martin," I said. "I've been shot. I've had to drain the blood from most of two meals, and frankly, I could use a nap. So I don't think it'd be best to let you out right now."

"Not let me out?" Incredulity was stamped across his face. "Isn't that why you're here? How did you find me?"

The adrenaline vanished from my body, and I could barely

stay standing. "I wasn't looking for you, Marty. I was looking for her. If I'd killed her upstairs, you would've been trapped down here and rotted, and we wouldn't be having this pleasant conversation."

"I'm too pretty to rot." Wow, his ego was the size of Manhattan. "Forgive me for being a little confused, but if you weren't sent to find me, then why were you hunting her?"

"That's classified," I said. It sounded official enough. "The people I work for didn't want me to know."

"You work for humans?"

I nodded.

His eyes narrowed. "You work for the bags of blood? Have you no couth?" He took a deep breath that made his nostrils flare. "You're a rogue are you? What's your family line?"

"That's my business. Not yours."

He guffawed. It was an aggravating sound. "Or, maybe you're just not properly educated. I thought we'd snuffed out the sympathizers. I guess not. There's always someone who goes against their true nature. Against the law. What's your name, little girl?"

"That's my business too," I said.

"Where did you grow up?" he asked.

"This isn't twenty questions, Bub." I must have been tired. I'd never used the word *bub* before. "And the more you pry, the less likely I am to let you out of the cage."

He slammed his hand against the window. The cell shook and seemed to move an inch toward me, but the glass held. "You're a traitor to your kind!" he shouted. "Let me give you a few facts. I am on day twenty-seven of my feeding cycle. In two days, I will need to feed. In three, I will go mad with bloodlust and tear myself to pieces. I am starving."

"Well, you can't eat me. I'm one of you."

This time his grin showed his incisors. "Oh, how little you know," he said. Vampires could eat vampires! I hadn't thought about that possibility. Or at least, I had dismissed it.

"Wait …" He placed his hand on the glass. "Look closely at me." I pulled my head back an inch or two. "Your eyes. They're gray."

"Whoopdedoo."

"Look at mine," he said. They were gray too. Something cold and snake-like began twisting in my gut.

"So what?" I said. "Eye color means nothing. Dominant genes tend to dominate."

"Well, Amber," he said. How the hell did he know my name? "I expect you to talk to me with much more respect. After all, you've been looking for me all your life."

"I have?" That gut snake had turned to ice.

"This is going to sound somewhat melodramatic: Amber Fang, I am your father."

I looked into his gray eyes. I swallowed.

"Shit," I said. "Shit. Shit. Shit."

24

Family Trees and Other Problems

I apologize for that last outburst. I try not to swear.

Unless I was in a fucking bad mood.

This whole "I am your father" thing was a gut punch of a revelation. There was something familiar about his face, and I recognized I had some of his features. The same chin. A pinched look to the eyes. So this was what Luke Skywalker felt like. Yes, I'd watched those movies. One had to if one wanted to understand the various human subcultures. I grok geeks. And eat them too.

"No," I said. "It can't be."

Again came his grating laugh. "Yes, it's the truth. Why didn't I see the likeness right away? My long-lost daughter, stolen from me by the sympathizer. How old are you now?"

"I—that's none of your business."

"Maybe you're twenty now. Twenty years of indoctrination. I don't know if that can be reversed. If you're here, then mommy can't be far away. Where is that little do-gooder?"

"That's classified information too."

"She works for these humans!" He scraped the glass with his fingernails. "For our food. She's gone beyond the pale. What did she teach you? Morality of the kill? Be kind to the kittens?" I knew part of the rant was fueled by his bloodlust. "I don't know why your mother grew so soft, or why I spent enough time with that bitch to father you."

"Don't call her that." My voice was weak.

"You won't understand this," he said, "but you're better than all of them. You're the nightmare in their tiny, mushy brains. We got rid of your mother's strain. Her parents. Her cousins. She was the last one. The dumb cow."

"She's not a cow!" I slammed my hand against the window, inches from his face, and he didn't even blink. That Johnny Depp-like grin just widened.

I collapsed into a nearby chair and spun so that my back was to him.

"I'm talking to you, Amber," he said. "Turn around. Right now." He was starting to sound like a dad.

I'd pictured this meeting several thousand times in my lifetime. It was *verboten* for Mom to mention him, so he had become a king in my memory. All she would say is, "You don't ever want to see him." But in my head, he'd save me from some dire event—a drowning or a fire or a gaggle of vampire slayers with stakes in hand. Or I would show him how high I could jump. Obviously, that was back when I was a kid. More recent daydreams involved me talking to him, learning the secrets my mother hadn't told me. And, yes, this was a cliché, but I dreamed that someday we would be a happy family again—like all those human families I saw on TV.

Mom was right. He wasn't worth meeting. It was like finding out your father was a bull snake.

Dermot came stumbling down the stairs. He was pale, and there was what looked like red syrup leaking from his neck. He surveyed the room and spotted Hallgerdur. Then he saw my father. Dermot's face went a little paler, and he stumbled over to me and placed his hand on my shoulder.

"How are you?" he asked.

"Peachy keen," I said. But I didn't lift up my head to meet his eyes.

"And who's that?" He motioned weakly.

"Is this the food you work with?" My father asked. "Is this blood bag on legs your boyfriend? Your partner? You couldn't even finish him off."

"That's my dad," I said. There was more than a little shame in my voice. "Welcome to my family reunion."

Dermot did give me the satisfaction of a shocked look and was speechless for a moment.

"He's a bit of an asshole, in case you hadn't guessed," I added.

"How do you know he's your father?"

"We have the same eyes. And he knew my name without me telling him."

"You get your hands off my little girl," my father said. "She's not your plaything, human."

"His name's Martin," I added.

Dermot nodded and gave my shoulder a squeeze. He walked over to the prison cubicle.

"Oh, here comes dinner," Dad said. "Wow, you don't even look like an aperitif. Get over here and give your daddy-in-law a big hug. Come on, you blood bag, come here, I—"

There was a *click.* I turned and saw that Martin was talking, but I couldn't hear him. "There's a silencer on these pens," Dermot said, pointing at a button.

"If only I'd known that a few minutes ago."

"I'm going to check on Hallgerdur." It sounded like a request.

133

"Go ahead. She was alive a few minutes ago."

He went over to his Icelandic ex-girlfriend and put his hand on her neck. "Still breathing. Low pulse. Nice tape job."

"Thanks. Mom was big on crafts." *Why aren't you here now, Mom?*

Dermot still had his hand on Hallgerdur's neck. "This was a very good day, Amber. It may not seem like it now. But it was."

I didn't care. I just needed to sleep.

He crossed his arms. "Now we just have to figure out how to get a pickup team in here. It'll be tricky, but I believe I have the answer."

25

First Class Ticket Home

We caught a helicopter ride to the nearby American Navy base and boarded a C-40A Clipper, a United States Navy jet. I only knew the name of the plane because Dermot kept talking about its capabilities and its history. The plane was the size of an average passenger plane, but the front had space for carrying "gear." The back half was your typical airplane seats, which was where we sat. Ten marines were seated ahead of us.

About five minutes later, a second helicopter *thup thup thupped* its way to the ground. They had somehow stuffed Dad into what looked to be a *Star Trek*-style, black metal coffin. They loaded him through a great big hatch at the front of the plane. An unconscious Hallgerdur was strapped to a gurney, a drip bag keeping her going. They carried her onto the plane and belted her down next to the coffin. A nurse in BDUs fussed over her.

Dermot had been given his own bag of plasma. The nurse popped by to check on him, and he managed a weak thumbs up.

His phone made an old-fashioned ringing sound. He looked at the screen and turned slightly paler.

"What is it?" I asked.

"Bad news," he said. "It's ... well, you don't have clearance for that information."

He put the phone away.

The plane growled into life and was soon grumbling through the air. I found my gaze drifting over to my father's coffin. Our whole exchange had lasted no longer than two minutes, but it had opened up a universe of questions. From what I could tell, every other vampire operated on a different moral code than I did. I'd read *Dracula* a few times. But I assumed we had evolved our moral compasses along with the humans. Apparently not.

What would it be like to not have to research every meal? To not have morals?

Was Mom the crazy one? No, Dad had mentioned sympathizers. So there once had been others.

And what had Mom seen in Dad? At one point, they must have had something in common.

My gut was still heavy with blood. My limbs and my head felt heavy too. It was getting too hard to think any logical thoughts. I closed my eyes, meaning only to take a nap.

It was with a bit of surprise that the shaking of the descending Clipper woke me, and I looked out the window to see we were approaching an airport. I'd slept for several hours.

"Welcome to Joint Base McGuire-Dix-Lakehurst in scenic New Jersey," Dermot said. I glanced over my shoulder to see that Hallgerdur was still strapped to her bed and fast asleep, and my father's steel coffin remained closed.

"So what are you going to do with my father?" I asked. I tried to make the question sound casual.

"That's not my decision." Dermot had some color back to his skin. There were still ugly black bags under his eyes.

"Thanks for the vague answer. Would you care to guess

what'll become of him?"

"We can keep him in stasis for a few weeks. Maybe months."

"And what does that do to his feeding cycle? He's supposed to eat in the next seventy-two hours."

"I honestly don't know, Amber. We're flying blind here. We could feed him."

"You mean just shove some old lady into his coffin?" My nails were puncturing the armrest.

"Old lady? No. I'm just telling you our options. He has information about the Grand Council."

"What's that?"

"We don't know a lot about the council. But somehow they run most of vampire society."

I filed that under *things I need to know more about.* "How would you get that information out of him? Waterboarding?"

"That wouldn't work."

"I was joking."

"I don't like the morals of it either, Amber. But what if the information he gives us can save lives? We have only vague conjecture about how many vampires are in the council, or where they are located."

"What would you do with that information? Hunt them down?"

"They aren't all like you, Amber."

I wasn't certain if that was a compliment. "You would kill my kind?"

"Our goal is to make the world a better place. That's all."

He must have taken a course on ambiguity. "Let's just stick to specifics, then. I don't like the idea of my father being experimented on. I just found him. And it's—it's not right."

Dermot could only manage a weak shrug.

"And what about Hallgerdur?" I asked.

"She'll be interrogated too."

"By you?"

"Again, I don't know. It'll be very difficult to get information out of her. But deals can be made. She may be more malleable in one of our safe rooms."

The conversation was interrupted by a rumbling as we landed on the tarmac and stopped near a hangar. The door on the side of the plane opened like a giant mouth. The marines lined either side of the ramp, and we proceeded out to where a black car and two black vans waited.

"Just once, I'd like to see a secret agency use pink vehicles," I said.

Dermot smiled, led me to the car, and got in on the other side. The prisoners were carried to the black vans. We left the military base. Soon we were out of the city and speeding along a highway.

"He may have the key to finding your mother," Dermot said, out of the blue. "Your father is a very important asset for us."

"Asset. Nice way to put it." I honestly couldn't explain the anger rising to the surface. Maybe it was the fact they would kill my own kind. Before I even got to know them. To know more about myself. "Will you promise me that I'll at least get to talk to him? Before you do whatever it is you do?"

"I'll put a request in on your behalf."

I rolled my eyes. "Where are we going?"

"You? Back to the White House. To study. To relax. Me? Maybe a hospital bed."

"You do realize that because of an interrupted feeding, my clock hasn't reset? I could snap into a bloodlust rage at any moment. I shouldn't have any visitors."

"We'll put a monitor on you," he said.

"There's a chance I'll go insane."

"Amber. I ... I didn't fully understand what I was asking. I shouldn't have interrupted you. I just couldn't let her go."

I bit my lip. It hurt when you had incisors like mine. "You mean emotionally?"

"No. I mean the information she has for the League."

The van turned right, and we zipped ahead. "Where are they going?" I asked.

"To a bunker."

"And will I see my father again?"

"As I said, I'll put in a request for you." His voice was weary. "Look, Amber, I don't have all the answers. The retrieval of both of these subjects represents a sea change in our information and how we'll operate in the future."

More time passed. I watched the scenery for a while. Like a long pan shot in a movie.

"Did you love her?" I asked.

"Yes. Long ago, I was a lot like her. I don't love her anymore. Not since she shot me."

"She shot you?"

"She was just proving her worth to ZARC by terminating our relationship."

"You make it sound so clinical."

He gave a shrug. "It's how I deal with it. And I shouldn't have survived. But it turns out I can be somewhat hard to kill."

All sorts of alarm bells were going off in my slow mind. "What does that mean?"

He waved a wavering hand. "Another story for another time."

A highway sign said *Welcome to Vermont.* Home sweet temporary home.

26

The White House Redux

The White House was the same as I'd left it. Dermot didn't get out of the car, but he patted my arm and said, "Good luck. Good work."

"I—I've never tried to kill you," I said. The words just came out. "At least not with all my heart."

That got a smile from him. Then I closed the door. Kato, or whatever his name was, led me to the house.

The concept of a bed was all my mind could handle. I wondered if Kato could defend himself from me. He was wearing a big honking Taser that looked like something out of a science fiction movie. I didn't know if that would be enough.

"Welcome home," he said.

I nodded, went into my room, dropped my bag, and fell onto the bed in a heap of Amber. I slept.

I didn't wake up for nearly twenty-four hours. When I did, I leapt out of bed and up the wall. I crawled upside down across the ceiling, dislodging chunks of stucco. For a moment, I saw red. A heartbeat later, it vanished.

I climbed down off the walls. Literally. And sat on the bed. It was still dark out, and I had a pounding headache. I was in a territory my mother had warned me about. *Always eat until the food is dead.* I pictured her waving her proverbial finger at me. *And clean up the dishes too.* But there was nothing I could do now. I was waiting for the feeding madness. From what I knew, one of two things could happen. I could snap and dine on whichever human I came across until sated, and then my clock would reset. Or, if no food was found, I might try to suck my own blood until I died.

It was 3:00 a.m. when I went to the kitchen and put coffee in the coffeemaker. It was an ancient, electric espresso cof-feemaker with an orange top. The percolating coffee percolated my brain to a slightly more awake state.

I sat in the rocking chair and read with hot coffee in hand, slowly rocking the whole time. I tried to remember my early years with Mom and how she would read to me, sometimes in a rocking chair, but most often in bed. I still had *Goodnight Moon* memorized. She'd even read *Harry Potter* to me when I was older.

I wished I could sit down with her now and have her tell me our story. How she had met Dad. Why she had left whatever vampire clan she was part of and what her reasons were. I could guess them, of course. But that wasn't the same as hearing a story firsthand.

Were there other moral vampires out there? Or was I a freak?

That was how I passed the night—thoughts of Mom and Dad and my place in the universe. It had been three days since my interrupted feeding. Maybe I should have kept a diary of my march to insanity. *Day three. I had coffee and read. I also climbed the ceiling.*

I went online and continued my classes, taking numerous notes for Information Access. My essay was waiting for me in

Word. I really preferred to deal with old books—antiquities and such—but this was knowledge I needed. After all, it was still my goal to become a full-time librarian. The way I felt at that moment, it looked much more attractive than charging across the world to dine on dangerous hit women and knife-wielding men.

I was too tired to train. The rest of my day was unmemorable. And so was the next, though I did dream about zebras.

I took more time to think about my father. By now, he might have been driven mad. Most likely, they had found a way to feed him. His attitude toward my mother and me was curious. As if *we* were the abominations. *He* was obviously the abomination. But what did I know of the rest of the vampire world?

On day six, a black car pulled into the driveway. I was lounging in a chair out front, in a jacket and under a blanket, reading *Misery*. I'd always kind of enjoyed reading while huddled under a blanket in the cold. I tried Anne Rice once, but really, those vampires would talk you to death.

The car sat still for several moments before the rear passenger window rolled down.

"Amber Fang?" The voice was female.

"Yes," I said, not making a motion to get up.

"Would you come here?"

"I prefer if you come here."

I sounded braver than I felt. I wasn't sure who was in there, and I'd had the slight hope it was Dermot until the woman spoke. The window rolled up. Several seconds passed. The door opened, and a black woman stepped out. She strode down the sidewalk, her long coat trailing behind her. She sat across from me and took off her black leather gloves.

"I'm Margaret Adams," she said. "I've been looking forward

to meeting you."

"I can't say I feel the same," I said. "Are you someone I should know?"

"I'm the chairman of the League."

"Oh. I met a different chairman earlier."

"We lost my predecessor." I remembered Hallgerdur spouting something about cutting off the head of the League. Had they killed Ernest? I'd only met him briefly, but had been impressed by his style.

"I—I'm sorry to hear that." I really did mean it. "He seemed like a nice guy."

"It's a challenging position." This was delivered flatly.

"I'm surprised you're out here on your own."

"I like to be hands on."

"I can appreciate that. So you must know about my father. What is he up to?"

"He continues in stasis." She sounded somewhat robotic.

"He's still sleeping in that coffin?"

"Yes. Have you experienced any mood swings?"

"A plethora. I could snap at any microsecond."

She patted her gloves on her knee. "Well, we're going to alleviate that situation."

"Is there a pill?"

"No. I've come to take you to a safer location."

"But I like this house. It's so ... white."

"You'll be returned to it. We've prepared a safe habitation zone for you."

I set down the coffee cup. Did everyone in this organization learn to speak by reading 1984? "What's to prevent you from locking me up forever?"

"You're too much of an asset. And we do have a contract with you."

"Why didn't you send Dermot to pick me up? He's your errand boy."

"Dermot has had a slight medical setback."

"Is he all right?" The concern peppering my voice surprised me.

"He'll recover. Now, did I mention that you'll have internet access in your new room?"

"Wow. And how will this solve the problem that I could snap at any time and begin a feeding frenzy?"

"I'll show you that when we arrive."

"Do I need to bring anything?"

"No."

I had a tingling Spidey sense that I should splash the remains of my coffee in her face and flee. But that was instinct rearing its instinctual head. Logic suggested I needed to have my feeding schedule reset. And, though I didn't quite trust her, I trusted Dermot.

So I followed Miss Adams to the car, bringing the book along. She even opened the door for me, which was rather kind. Then she sat on the opposite side. The driver was an Indian man, his turban black. She said something in Hindi, and we started down the road.

Then we were quiet, and eventually, I started to read again. It wasn't that long of a drive, maybe two hours. Or another eighty pages in my book, which was how I often measured time. She said something to the driver in Hindi again, and all the windows, including the one between us and the driver, went black, along with the interior of the car.

Margaret hit a switch and the light above me turned on. "What's this about?" I asked.

"Well, we can't have you knowing exactly where home base is."

We turned to the right. A sharp turn.

"I guess that makes sense." Though the sensation of moving through absolute darkness was unnerving. We turned to the right.

"You can keep reading, if you like."

I did so. Another hour passed. We suddenly went down an incline, and the windows became see-through again. We were in a long tunnel, lights on. Soon, we came to an underground parking lot. More black cars than I could shake a stick at. We then stopped in a parking spot marked *Chairman*.

"Come with me," she said. We exited the car. "Welcome to home base."

If this was their office building, I pitied them. Never had I seen so much dull lighting and gray cinderblock. I didn't know what I had expected. I guess my imagination had been fed by all the spy movies with glass elevators, black pods opening up, and walls swishing out of sight to reveal secret rooms.

Instead, there was a beat-up elevator with orange doors and an orange interior. Ugly orange, I might add. And the further down it went, the more the air smelled like rotten fruit. When the doors opened, there were more gray walls. It had all the pleasantness of a Cold War-era morgue in Russia.

"Was there a sale on gray paint?" I asked.

She graced me with a look most people would save for a bird that had defecated on their windshield. "Come this way, Amber," she said.

I followed her into an office that housed about fifteen cubicles and the same number of geeks. There were three security guards in nondescript outfits patrolling the hallway. "This is where it all happens," she said.

"Interesting," I said, though it was the opposite. No outrageously handsome secret agents. Most everyone had glasses and that pale look people got from lack of sun exposure. Several of the desks had typewriters. I guess Dermot wasn't kidding about their old tech.

"Come along." She continued through the main office and down another hallway.

A few of the office workers looked up at me. It dawned on me that several of them may have been spending the last few years staring at my photograph, reading my file, and falling in love with me. I winked at one particularly lonely looking male, and he blushed.

In the next room, recognition lit up the synapses in my brain. "Jordan Rex," I said. "I'd know that face anywhere." He was the very first contact, the man I'd pursued in Seattle, who had turned out to be a League agent. "Or is Jordan your real name?"

"It's not." He didn't blink. I'd file him under *I'm not happy we have a vampire in our employ.*

"Michael Hexdall, allow me to introduce Amber ..." She paused. "Which last name are you using now?"

"Fang," I said.

Michael nodded. "It's good to meet you again."

Margaret gestured, and we went down a long hallway with closed door after closed door on each side of us, each with a number on it. Then the hallway opened up into a larger room.

There were about twenty holding cells here. Uneasiness settled in my brain. "Where exactly are you taking me?"

"The sunshine room," she answered.

To my utter stunnification, the walls of the next hall were painted with soothing sunlight and cloud scenes. Did they have

146

daycare here? She opened up a pink metal door. Yes, pink. We went inside.

At first, I thought we'd somehow magically climbed to the surface, for there was a prairie scene in front of me, the sun in the distance. Birds chirped. A couch sat near the window. I blinked. Then it became clear that a large HD screen made up one wall.

Dermot was sitting in a black chair, his skin still rather pale but speckled with pink. He looked better than he had a few days ago. I guess they'd squirted a few blood products into him.

"Hi, Amber," he said. "Welcome to the sunshine room. Your new home."

27

All Is Not Sunny in the Sunshine Room

"Home?" I echoed. "Huh?"

Sometimes I slipped into complete ineloquence. I blamed it on running from trailer park to trailer park.

"We're worried about your reset date," he said.

"You mean, when my biological clock will demand a feeding."

"Yes. I interrupted it. And so, to make amends, I convinced the League that you deserved your own room."

"Do I get to snack on you?"

"Been there. Bled there. Not again."

I licked my lips.

"We brought you here," Margaret said, "because this is a comfortable, contained place for you to wait for this reset to occur. I'm sure you'll adapt to your new surroundings."

"I can adapt to anything," I said. "But what am I supposed to do here for fun?"

"You have a nice view." Dermot tapped a button on a remote and a jungle came up followed by jungle sounds. Soon, I'd be meditating to ocean waves. "There is a bed." He got up, flicked a switch, and a bed came out of the wall. It was one long, black mattress and looked rather comfortable. "You have a coffee machine. You don't need food. Well, our food. There's an en suite shower through that door. And plenty of books." He gestured toward a shelf. "Plus, you'll be able to connect to your online classes."

"Sounds so very pleasant." I touched a few of the books on the shelf.

"I know it's not perfect," Margaret said, ignoring my sarcasm. "You'll have to trust us that it's best for you."

"You didn't consult me."

"We wanted to show you first. We expected a negative reaction."

I looked around the room. "Does that TV get HBO?"

Dermot shrugged. "We can bring in movies on a USB stick. Any requests?"

"*Escape from Alcatraz.* Or *Shawshank Redemption.*"

His smile made wrinkles form around his eyes and for the first time, I thought I saw scar tissue there. From surgery, perhaps.

"How long will I be here?"

"That depends on when you reset," Margaret said.

"Yes, I suppose it does. Is there a plan in place for after the reset happens? A visit to a prison, perhaps?"

Margaret tapped on a second door in the wall. It was black and metal and very thick. "That door will open. A woman or a man will walk through. You will be fed."

"I'll be living right beside my food?"

She nodded. "The subject will be comfortable. We'll provide you with files to prove said subjects conform to your moral code as it relates to eating."

"Will my future victims know?" I asked.

She shook her head. "No sense causing psychological trauma."

"You'd better provide reliable documents."

"We will," Margaret said. "I'll leave you in Dermot's capable hands." Then she was up and out of the room. My room. My feeding pen.

"How have you really been, Amber?" Dermot asked when the door closed behind her

"Agitated. Sleepless. On edge."

"So, the same as always."

I gave him a half-hearted smile. "And you, Dermie?"

He raised an eyebrow at this pet name. "I'm well enough. Did actually get to have a few days off. I even went to a baseball game."

"Oh, visit your folks? Turkey dinner?"

"My folks are under the impression I'm dead."

I nodded. He was all in, in terms of this organization. "Well, that's sad," I said softly. I know it could have been interpreted as sarcasm. "So what's happened with your girlfriend?" I asked.

"That's classified. You know that."

"A girl can ask."

"I want to know how you feel, Amber. Are you thinking about feeding more often?"

"Why?"

"Because I'm worried about you. About ... well ... your condition."

"You make it sound like I'm pregnant."

He shrugged. "You've never been in this situation. I've seen the blood madness once."

"And what happened?"

"It was four years ago. We had one of your kind as a prisoner. And, well, we didn't know about the feeding cycle."

"Male or female?"

He hesitated. "Female. But it wasn't your mother, if that's what you're asking. She was ancient. She looked a thousand years old. And she was missing three fingers on her left hand."

"Who was she?"

"The name she gave us was Carpetha. Our best guess was that she was one of the Grand Council." He ran a hand through his hair. "She hated us, Amber. I mean, I know you dislike humans, but I do sense a fraction of respect. But this one … even the sight of us was anathema to her. She tore the heads off of three of our men. Right in front of me."

"What happened to her?"

"We drove her back into her holding cell. I shocked her. Enough to kill a bull. She went mad a few hours later. She threw herself against the walls of the cubicle until it was a big blood smear. Biting at the walls, gouging out the cement. Then she started to bite her own arms. Any place she could reach with her teeth. She bled to death."

I swallowed. "She bit herself?"

"There wasn't much left. 'The thirst!' she shouted. So this is …. uh … territory I don't want you to explore."

"It's not territory I want to be in. But I have fed a little. Perhaps that changes the equation."

"That's my hope. We are on day seven of your interrupted feed. But there really is no way to know when your internal clock will reset. I assume it's not a sudden clicking over, that you'll have some sort of warning."

"Maybe you should visit me via Skype."

"I'm confident you'll be able to control yourself. At first, anyway."

"I'll do my very best," I said. "That's a promise."

28

The Interminable Joy of Waiting

The waiting was not pleasant.

Dermot visited me in the afternoons. At least, I assumed it was afternoon. I only had the clocks to judge by. I was beginning to miss the sight of the sun, the warmth of rays on my skin. I got tired of breathing air that had been pumped a thousand yards down a shaft into this room.

I paced the room clockwise, counterclockwise, and clockwise again. There were several cameras watching me. I would literally climb the walls and hang from the ceiling and look right into one of them every once in a while. I could only imagine the startled lackey on the other side. I watched the door to the outer office waiting for Dermot to arrive. I watched a season of *Friends*. It was quaint what people used to find funny.

I stared at the black door, too, and would stand nonchalantly beside it. I didn't hear any voices, though. Perhaps they didn't talk to anyone or to themselves, or else they just didn't talk. Could have been a mute. Or a monk. Or a ninja. I couldn't hear a heartbeat.

That didn't mean there wasn't one. Just that I couldn't hear it. And I wanted to. I needed to.

I paced. And played solitaire. And watched the time tick down each day as I waited for Dermot to appear. He would visit me on the hour at 3:00 p.m. My thoughts were not flipping toward blood, nor was I staring at his jugular any more than I had any other time. Boredom ruled the kingdom of my mind.

I couldn't help but wonder if there were cameras in the shower. Some pimply geek was just aching to get his thrills, I bet. Maybe even itching to upload the video to vampirenude.com. I scoured the tiny bathroom looking for a camera. I crawled over every space and found nothing. Finally, I unscrewed the light bulb and showered in the dark. Unless they had an infrared camera, they had no visual access to my private bits.

I wasn't usually so prim and proper, but there was a difference between showing your body willingly and being forced to show it.

Each day, I'd sit near the black door for longer and longer periods. Listening. Licking my lips.

"I need the paperwork," I told Dermot on the following visit. "I might snap at any time, so I need to know who's on the other side of the door."

"The research department is slow with the paperwork. It's been delayed."

"How can it be delayed?"

"This was a sudden situation. It's not like we had planned ahead to have you in this room. Please be patient."

"You know me, Dermie. I'm not the patient sort."

"That's for certain."

I angrily curled an eyebrow. "You're not the one locked in here. I need to know who my next meal is. Now!"

"I've been pushing for it. You'll have it by tomorrow."

"I hope that's soon enough."

"I understand your frustration," he said. "And I do look forward to getting you back into the field."

"It's open sky I want to see. I'm suffocating here."

"We're doing the best we can."

"Well, do better." Then I whispered, "I feel I am going mad."

"But are you thinking of feeding? Is that it?"

There was no hunger in my stomach. "No. Just. Getting out."

He put his hand on my shoulder. For whatever reason, his touch actually calmed me. "You're going to make it through this, Amber. You're the toughest woman I know."

I breathed in. "Thanks, Dermot. I appreciate it."

After he left, I played solitaire again. Then I read *The Stand* and a John Green novel. Oh, and I studied. They'd been kind enough to bring me a few of my textbooks. And finally, I turned out the lights. Red lights appeared on the ceiling—a smoke detector and cameras—the crimson stars of my sky. I paced in the dark, the room memorized. I settled myself against the metal door and listened. Why did they have these two suites side by side? Had they done this before?

I listened.

And I heard crying. My food next door was weeping. Not the wailing of a mourning parent. But the quiet snuffling of, say, someone who had just broken up with their boyfriend.

Paperwork! I nearly shouted. Or maybe I did shout it.

The person on the other side might actually be experiencing some sort of regret.

I certainly was.

29

Blood Red Blood

The following day was my last in the Sunshine Room. I woke up bone and flesh tired and wondering whether the crying I'd heard had been my imagination. I began by pacing, then I sat and fidgeted while I read about the use of vellum for books, then I paced again. Paced. Paced. At 3:00 p.m., Dermot's usual visiting time, the red door did not open. I glared at it, willing him to come in. Perhaps I could tear it off its hinges. No. I'd have trouble getting through that much reinforced steel. I was having difficulty breathing, and it crossed my mind that the League had perhaps grown tired of me and had cut off the air. Oxygen and blood, my two loves.

I dabbed at the sweat on my forehead.

The second hand clicked by, but the minute hand refused to budge much more than a micrometer.

Four o' clock. Dermot was late—much later than he'd been any other day. What could have delayed him?

And where was the paperwork?!

There was more crying from the other room. I jumped to the door, landed silently, and listened. No. It was my imagination. No noise.

What if the hunger came and there was no food here?

I crawled up the ceiling and stared in a camera, hissing, "Where's Dermot? Send him in here. Now."

Then I dropped down to the floor again. Pacing.

I did the same thing to another camera. And another. I went to all twelve of them.

For a moment, the whole room went red. Then it all flipped back to normal, as if an eye doctor had flicked a lens in front of my eye. The color was right. Proper.

And again it flicked. Red. Red. Red. Painting the room.

Then back again. I put my hands to my head. A scream of rage bubbled closer and closer to the surface. I squeezed, and that slowed it.

Then red again. Just like that. And when it came back, the clock was ten minutes ahead.

The table was broken.

I looked around. Someone else had been in here. Had broken the table and punched the screen on the wall, cracking it in several places. I ran from one corner of the room to another, into the washroom, the shower.

No one was here. No one but me. No scent.

I stood in the center of the room. Breathing slowly. Deeply. Calming myself. I'd broken the table and the TV. It was me. Somehow.

Red again. Red. Red. Red.

Twenty minutes passed. The couch had been shredded.

I hadn't moved from the center of the room. But of course, I had done it all. And I was sweating like a pig. I knew pigs didn't sweat. Neither did I. Most of the time.

Then another ticking sound, like the door of a safe opening. The black door.

The one between the two rooms.

I didn't dare move. I sniffed and smelled the scent of a human being. The delicate aroma went straight to my head. I momentarily thought all would go red again.

They were letting my meal in.

"H-hello?" a female voice said. She peeked in. The door was at least a foot thick. "Hello?"

I said nothing. But I could hear her heart beating slightly faster. She'd showered recently, used strawberry shampoo. I did not twitch a muscle. I waited in the center of the room. Every nerve ending on my fingers tingled. Each muscle prepared to pounce.

She was a sprite of a woman, white pale skin with dark hair and wide eyes. In a white blouse and pants. Why would they dress her in sacrificial white? It made feeding messier.

And made me hungrier. I didn't know why.

"Who-who are you?" she asked.

"Go back to your room," I whispered.

She stared at me. Did not move.

Then to the cameras I said, "I need papers. I need proof!"

"Please tell me who you are," she said.

"You start. What's your name?"

"S-Susan." She looked like a Susan. I didn't know what that meant, but she did look like a Susan. She seemed normal. Not a killer.

"I'm Amber," I spat the words. My voice was ragged. Her heartbeat was slightly elevated. I licked my lips. "Who have you killed?"

"Killed? No one. Did someone say I killed someone? I haven't."

"Why were you in that room?"

"I was told to wait there. They said I'd be released if I was good."

"Who are 'they'?"

"I don't know. Some men in gray suits picked me up off the street. I was walking to the post office. I was mailing letters to my mother. And my father. They're in a retirement home in Tampa Bay. Then a black van squealed to a stop, and the men grabbed me, put a black bag over my head, and brought me here."

Her heartbeat hadn't sped up during her recounting of the episode.

"What do you do for a living?" I asked.

"I'm a dental assistant. For Dr. Mueller. He does cosmetic dentistry. Smile makeovers, veneers. Why all these questions?"

This wasn't adding up. Why would they put a civilian in here? The League wouldn't just scoop someone up off the street. They weren't that type of organization. Unless I was reading them wrong.

The room went red for a moment.

Susan's eyes were wide. "Do you always swear that much?"

"Swear? I wasn't swearing. What are you talking about?"

"You did. Swears that I can't repeat. And you said someone's name. Dermot."

"Dermot?" I clenched a fist, my nails digging into my palm.

"Is that a boyfriend?"

I refrained from slapping her. "No. Never. An extremely annoying human. Go back to your room."

"But why are you here? Why are we prisoners?"

"I'm not a prisoner." The words sounded false. "This is just a temporary home."

I wiped another splash of sweat from my forehead. It dripped down into my eyes, stinging enough to make me blink.

"Are you certain you're all right?" Susan asked.

"I'm fine!"

Again, her heartbeat didn't quicken. I should've found that curious. I was having difficulty holding my thoughts together. Putting them in line one after another. They were. Order. Out of. What was her name again? Susan. Susan.

"You seem to be perturbed," she said. Her teeth were perfectly white. But she *was* a dental hygienist.

"I'm far beyond being perturbed."

"Well, how do we get out of here?"

"Get the fuck back to your room!"

The room flashed red. My thoughts fled. When I came to, they flocked back to me. Susan was in the corner. Hiding behind a chair.

"Are you done?" she asked.

There were holes ripped in the roof. I had pried five of the cameras out of their slots. They hung in various states of destruction. Lights blinking. Every book in the room had been torn to shreds. I had damaged books!

"I don't know," I said. The sweat. The sweat. The sweat. I never sweated. Why was this happening?

"Can I stand up now?" She raised her head a little, reminding me of a meerkat. Her neck was so perfectly bare.

"Do whatever you want."

"You ... you threatened me several times. And ... and in your mouth. I've never seen teeth like that."

For the third time, I noted that her heartbeat hadn't accelerated. If I'd been threatening her, she should have manifested all the signs of fear. Freaking the shit out. Instead, she was

159

calm. If I'd flashed my fangs, a normal human female would have peed her panties.

"You're not a dental assistant," I said.

"I am. I work for Dr. Mueler. On Seventh Street."

"No. You're too calm. It's as if all of this is normal for you."

She shook her head. "I'm not lying to you, Amber. I wouldn't lie. My mother taught me better than that."

"Your mother in the retirement home. Yes. And your father. In Florida. Details that you've given me. Are they real?"

"Of course they are." She ran a hand through her hair. "I loved them. I love them. Why won't you believe me?"

"Because you're too calm. You've just had your life threatened, and you sit as calm as … as …" Words were flowing around my brain, but I couldn't grab one. A flower? A turtle? "You're just too calm."

Her eyes narrowed the slightest bit. "I am who I say I am. I never lie."

"No. Why are you here? Your story seems so …" Stupid words. They were failing to flap into my brain. I'd read dictionaries from cover to cover. "…contrived."

"I'm a fellow agent," she said quietly. "They got sick of me. So they put me in here beside you."

"Who are you?"

"Susan. That's my name. But I'm a systems analyst. That's what I do. Always looking at numbers. I help plan your … your … missions."

"My dining expeditions," I said.

"Oh. Yes, them. I plan them. I do. All the best restaurants."

There was a crackling above me. So loud my ears hurt. I clamped my hands over them.

When I removed my hands, Chairperson Margaret's voice

160

came from a tinny speaker, "She's a killer, Amber. You have a green light. Go."

"I want paperwork!" I shouted. "I don't eat without paper-work."

In retrospect, that demand sounded ridiculous. But I did need to know.

"What do you mean, 'eat'?" Susan asked.

I pointed at her. "You. Shut up." Then I jammed a finger at the nearest camera. "Come in here, Dermot. Come in here now!"

"He can't come in there, Amber," Margaret said, her voice still crackling. "He's not here right now."

"Not here! Then show me the papers. I want a file."

"We can't provide files at this moment. You have to trust me, Amber. She's a grifter, a very gifted one, and she's playing you. She killed her parents first. She fits your moral criteria."

She sounded like a bureaucrat. Like I was asking for my taxes.

"Who are you talking to?" Susan asked. Then a heartbeat later. "I didn't kill my parents. I loved them. Love them."

"I don't know exactly who I'm talking to," I said. The statement rang with truth.

Susan turned toward the speaker. "Hey! There's been a mistake. You have the wrong person in here." Then she looked at me. "The wrong people."

"She killed a male senior citizen," Miss CEO said. "In Memphis. When her grifting went wrong."

"What?!" Susan said. "This is all lies. You have the wrong person. Let me go."

But her heartbeat was not speeding up.

"Did you do those things?" I asked.

"Never," Susan said. "I've never even been to Tennessee.

I'm one of you. We're both prisoners here. We have to work together."

"Did you ever feel regret?" I asked.

She opened her mouth, but her reply was drowned by a roar in my ears. I was going red again. A sudden shift in my eyes, over my senses. And then.

She put up her hand. She ran from me. A blow. A river of red. Her carotid artery.

Her red came out.

And into me.

30

Sleep, Perchance to Dream

I slept for three days. Then I rose. I knew it sounded religious. But it wasn't. I was shaking like a leaf in a breeze of anger. I was in a white hospital gown and on a gurney. Someone had changed my clothes without my consent. Someone had touched me! And put this horrible, scratchy goddamned gown on me.

I'd slept in the presence of humans.

I tried to sit up, but straps held me down, and there was an IV beside me—a pale liquid dripping into my bloodstream.

A nurse with a surgical mask came into my vision, and her eyes widened. "The subject is awake," she said.

I thought she was talking to me. But it was into a small communicator on the wall.

"The subject is pissed!" I shouted.

It didn't come out like that. In fact, the words didn't come out at all. Just a blast of slurred syllables.

"Where am I?" I asked. More slurring. "What's going into my arm?" Those words did come out clearly, and the nurse nodded.

"A blood substitute. An adjusted glycol. Doctor Einer thought it would be help to reset your ... um ... how to put it?"

"Your clock," another voice finished.

Then Dermot was above me. I was hit with the need to both kiss and scratch his face. Neither happened.

"Get it out of my arm," I spat.

"Not yet, Amber. It's balancing your system. Well, as far as we understand your system. How do you feel?"

"Undo these straps and find out."

He smiled that Boy Scout smile of his. "Yes. Well, we can't quite do that yet. I want to be sure you're back to normal."

"I feel like scratching your eyeballs out. Normal enough?"

"You *are* feeling better. Have you had any more red episodes?"

Things came back to me. A destroyed room. Susan. The redness. It was all a long time ago. Distant. Almost as if someone else had done it.

"No. What happened to Susan?"

"You fed," he said quietly. "And then you fell down and have been in stasis for the last three days."

"Stasis?"

"Well, more like a coma. We did a few blood tests, and from what we understand of your chemistry, it's back to normal. We believe your clock is reset."

"You poked needles into me?"

He shrugged. "We had to, Amber."

"And why didn't you have paperwork on Susan? Why didn't you have proof?"

"We were still working on her case. We had circumstantial evidence. Her DNA was found at crime scenes where it shouldn't have been found. So we were ninety-five percent convinced. But proof moves slow in our world."

"Did she regret her murders?" I asked.

"I—I don't know."

"Well that's kind of an important distinction to me." Dermot said nothing. "And where were you? Why was your boss talking to me?"

"I ..." A long pause. He looked toward one of the cameras on the wall and back to me. "I was detained."

"You sure picked a convenient time to be detained. I needed you. I needed you. To talk. Talk." Why was I repeating things? "Why am I repeating things?"

"You may still be adjusting to your medications."

"There are medications too?"

"Yes, just something to calm you down. It's a cousin to the sedative we used on you in our first encounter."

"I'm not a lab rat!" Then the realization. "You took samples, didn't you?" There were several needle marks on my arms.

"We did tests. You weren't harmed."

"Shouldn't I have a choice?"

"Calm down, Amber." He leaned a little closer, and I strained at my leather arm bands. "You couldn't expect us not to test you. And what we learn, well, it can be used. Perhaps to save your father."

"And what you learn could be used against me. And my kind."

"I realize trust has to be built up again. We made a mistake."

"Several mistakes. She didn't get a chance to express her remorse. I shouldn't have eaten her."

"I know. We messed up. But we saved you, Amber. The clock is reset. You're back to normal."

"You put me in this situation. All because you wanted to save your girlfriend."

"There were reasons, good reasons."

My brain was liquefied jelly, and my thoughts were tadpoles. Angry tadpoles. But I bit my tongue. "I need to sleep," I said.

"Or I may see red again."

"Then sleep, Amber. We'll talk again when you feel more energetic."

I slept.

And by slept, I meant I went for another fifteen hours without waking. Who knows what they poked me with during that time? But I was refreshed when I awakened. The same nurse was there. My headache was gone. The toilet bowl of my thoughts was clear.

"I'm checking out," I said. My voice was surprisingly steady, though my throat felt a little ragged.

"What?" the nurse said.

I curled my wrist back and cut through the bands on my right arm. They'd obviously forgotten about my beautiful, perfect nails. I reached across and cut my other bonds. "Please keep your hands away from the alarm or the speaker phone."

"You're on camera," she said.

"No, I'm not." I leapt, pulled the camera out of the ceiling, and landed on my feet. It felt rather good. Maybe the stuff they'd given me was making me stronger. Faster. Smarter.

Woozier. A wave of nausea came over me. Then I straightened and got control of myself again. "I'm checking out," I repeated. "I won't hurt anyone if they don't stop me."

Nurse Blondie backed out of my way. There was a door, but it was unlocked, and I opened it. Then I walked down a hallway. "I won't hurt anyone," I said, certain I was on camera each step of the way. "I promise."

Guards appeared at the end of the hall, hands on their holstered guns. They looked uncertain of their orders. I strode calmly toward them. There was too much to sort out. My father was here, perhaps in another bunker. My mother was gone. I

door. The
I was o
And I w

couldn't fully trust Dermot or any of them. I was muddled. I needed to tease out the details.

I heard the words, "Let her pass," come out of one man's earphone thingy. The guards backed out of my way. "Thank you, boys," I said.

Their heartbeats were slightly elevated. They'd been well trained.

I opened that door and strode into the orange elevator. I pressed the M button, and a few moments later, the door opened into the analyst room.

The geeks had fled. Their typewriters still had papers in them, reports half composed. Warm coffees still sat on their desks. Obviously, I'd set off some evacuation protocol. Now which way was out? They wouldn't just let me go, would they? I expected some show of force.

Down a hallway, I found another elevator. And up, up, up it went. Apparently once you were inside the building, you could leave. You just couldn't get in without a key card. Or they had let me go through.

The door opened into the parking lot. I walked out.

Dermot was sitting on a black car.

"I should have known you'd be here," I said.

"Amber, please reconsider what you're doing."

"I'm returning to my normal life," I said. "One where I am not tested, where I am not put in a pen next to my meal, where there are people I can trust." Well, there was no place with that last bit. "I'm done, Dermis." Yes, I had just called him "skin."

"No. We've accomplished so much in such a short time. And there is so much more we could do."

"I need to clear my thoughts. I need space. I need normalcy—my type of normalcy. To sort out what I want for my life. A

gone a

"We

that nc

"Yes

I smile

He di

they co

Final

"You

"No.

"The:

He wa

It did

gas wou

"Take

for seve

a fifty fi

"And

The da

There re

"Keep

knockec

accelera

nothing

Time ⌐

the mot

several l

When

light. Th

darkene

About the Author

Arthur Slade was raised in the Cypress Hills of southwest Saskatchewan and began writing at an early age. He is the author of nineteen books, including DUST (which won the Governor General's award), FLICKERS and THE HUNCHBACK ASSIGNMENTS (which won the Grand prix de L'Imaginaire). He currently lives in Saskatoon, Canada. Visit him online at: www.arthurslade.com